SAFARI SURVIVOR

OWEN M. SMITH & ANNE COLLINS SMITH

ILLUSTRATED BY RUBINE

GRAPHIC UNIVERSE™ • MINNEAPOLIS • NEW YORK

Story by Owen M. Smith and Anne Collins Smith

Pencils and inks by Rubine

Coloring by Studio Rubine

Lettering by Felix Ruiz

Graphic Universe
A division of Lerner Publishing Group, Inc.
241 First Avenue North
Minneapolis, MN 55401 U.S.A.

Website address: www.lernerbooks.com

Main body text set in Myriad Tilt Bold 14/16. Typeface provided by Adobe Systems.

Library of Congress Cataloging-in-Publication Data

Smith, Owen (Owen M.)
    Safari survivor / by Owen Smith and Anne Smith ; illustrated by Rubine.
        p.   cm. — (Twisted journeys ; #21)
        Summary: On safari in Tanzania, the reader is asked to make choices throughout the story to avoid becoming breakfast for a hungry lion.
    ISBN 978–0–7613–6727–7 (lib. bdg. : alk. paper)
        1. Plot-your-own stories. 2. Graphic novels. [1. Graphic novels. 2. Safaries—Fiction. 3. Survival—Fiction. 4. Adventure and adventurers—Fiction. 5. Tanzania—Fiction. 6. Plot-your-own stories.] I. Smith, Anne (Anne Collins) II. Rubine, ill. III. Title.
    PZ7.7.S644Saf 2012
    741.5'973—dc23   2011039798

Manufactured in the United States of America
1 – PP – 12/31/11

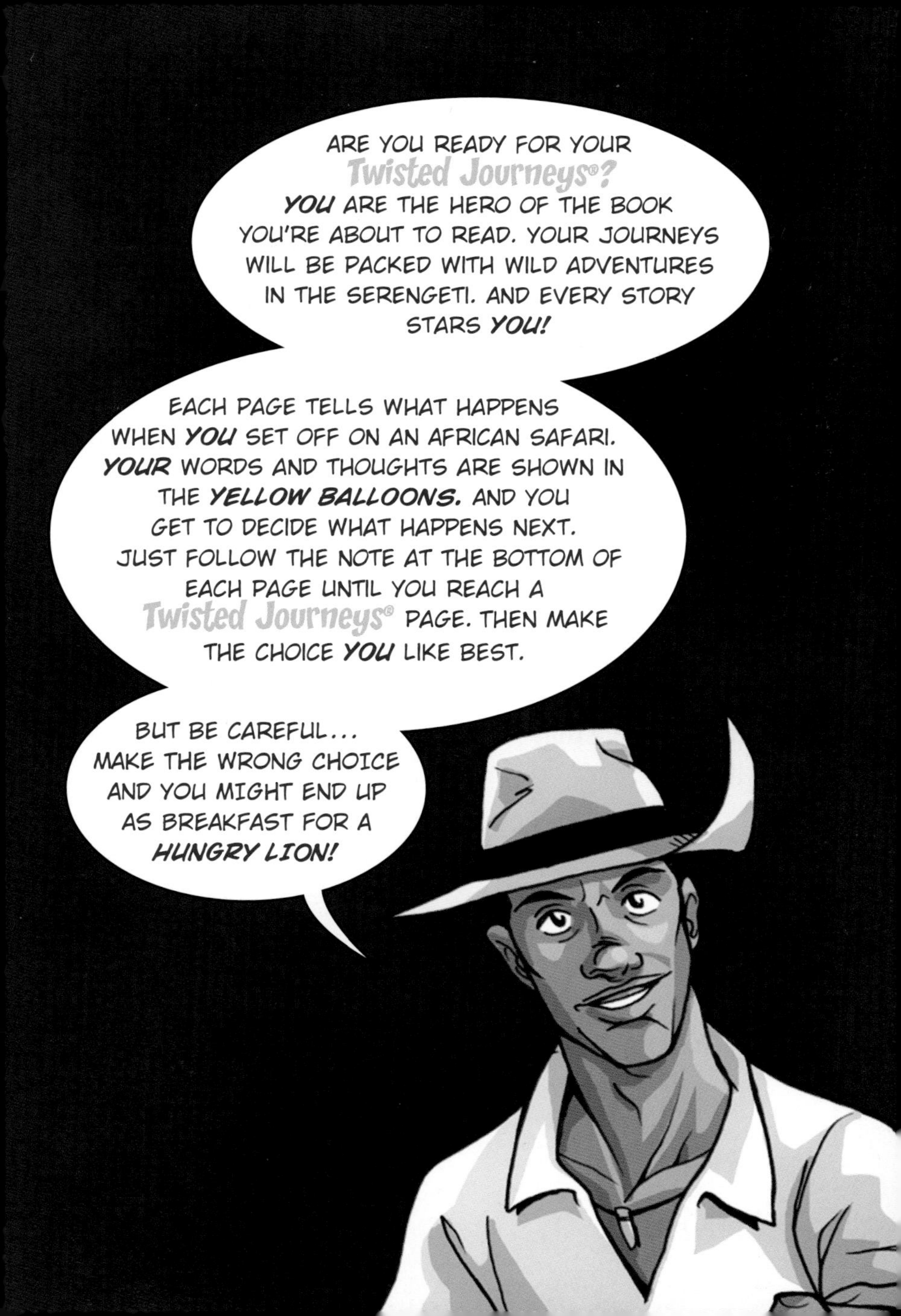

ARE YOU READY FOR YOUR Twisted Journeys®? YOU ARE THE HERO OF THE BOOK YOU'RE ABOUT TO READ. YOUR JOURNEYS WILL BE PACKED WITH WILD ADVENTURES IN THE SERENGETI. AND EVERY STORY STARS YOU!
EACH PAGE TELLS WHAT HAPPENS WHEN YOU SET OFF ON AN AFRICAN SAFARI. YOUR WORDS AND THOUGHTS ARE SHOWN IN THE YELLOW BALLOONS. AND YOU GET TO DECIDE WHAT HAPPENS NEXT. JUST FOLLOW THE NOTE AT THE BOTTOM OF EACH PAGE UNTIL YOU REACH A Twisted Journeys® PAGE. THEN MAKE THE CHOICE YOU LIKE BEST.
BUT BE CAREFUL... MAKE THE WRONG CHOICE AND YOU MIGHT END UP AS BREAKFAST FOR A HUNGRY LION!

The setting sun glares down on you as a bead of sweat trickles down your neck. You can't believe it gets this hot in March! But it makes sense—you're close to the equator.

You're in Tanzania for an African safari with your family. You're going to be missing some school, but your teacher said it would be okay, as long as you brought back some good stories and pictures to share with the class.

Still, you're looking forward to encountering wild animals, both familiar and unfamiliar. You've been to zoos before, but there the animals were always in enclosures or behind barriers. Here there won't be anything between you and the animals. You'll get to see wild animals that are truly in the wild.

GO ON TO THE NEXT PAGE.

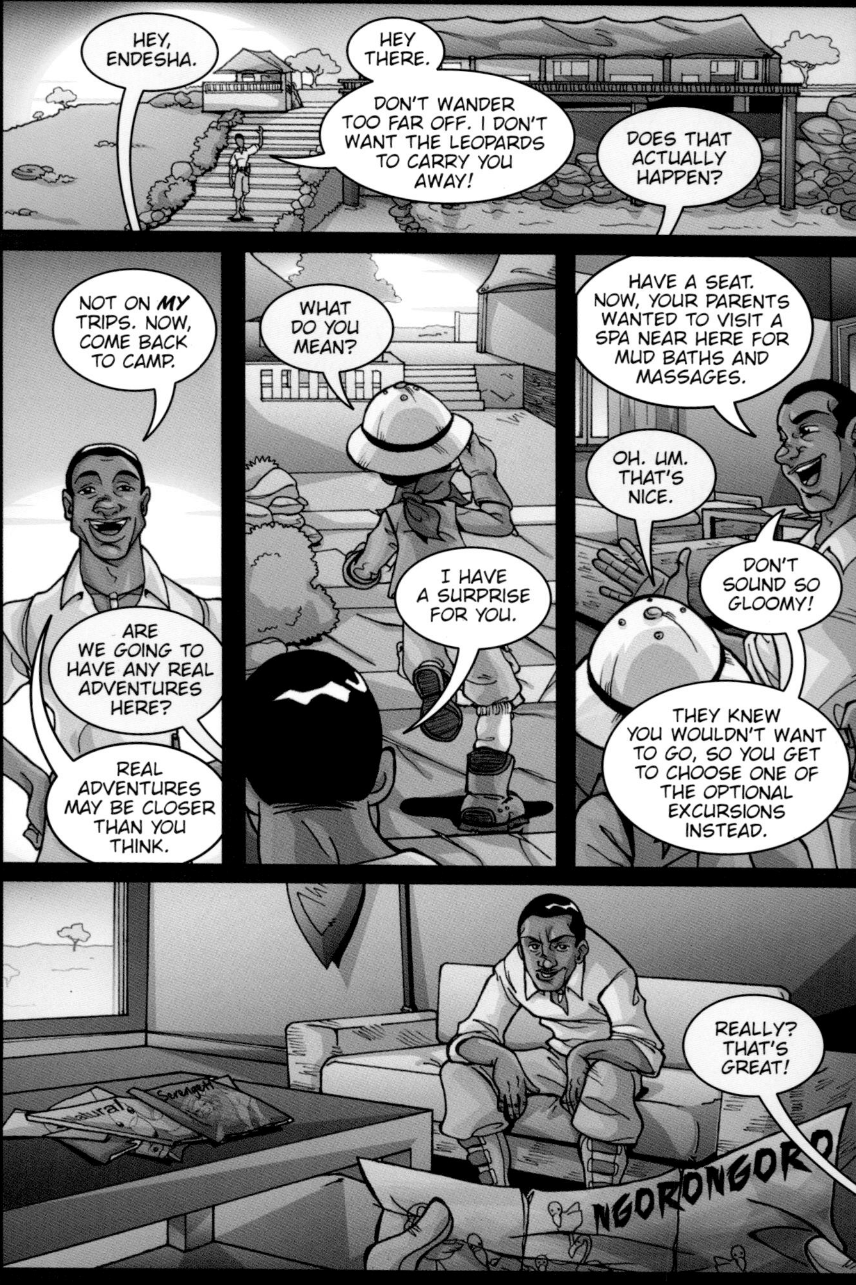
HEY, ENDESHA.
HEY THERE.
DON'T WANDER TOO FAR OFF. I DON'T WANT THE LEOPARDS TO CARRY YOU AWAY!
DOES THAT ACTUALLY HAPPEN?
NOT ON *MY* TRIPS. NOW, COME BACK TO CAMP.
ARE WE GOING TO HAVE ANY REAL ADVENTURES HERE?
REAL ADVENTURES MAY BE CLOSER THAN YOU THINK.
WHAT DO YOU MEAN?
I HAVE A SURPRISE FOR YOU.
HAVE A SEAT. NOW, YOUR PARENTS WANTED TO VISIT A SPA NEAR HERE FOR MUD BATHS AND MASSAGES.
OH. UM. THAT'S NICE.
DON'T SOUND SO GLOOMY!
THEY KNEW YOU WOULDN'T WANT TO GO, SO YOU GET TO CHOOSE ONE OF THE OPTIONAL EXCURSIONS INSTEAD.
REALLY? THAT'S GREAT!
NGORONGORO

GO ON TO THE NEXT PAGE.

Endesha explains your choices. "You can visit the Ngorongoro Conservation Area, which offers a great variety of terrain. It has a volcano, a salt lake, a world-famous dig with early human fossils, and grasslands filled with all kinds of birds and animals.

"Or you can explore the Serengeti National Park. This time of year there will be many young animals, and you can see great herds of wildebeest, zebra, and antelopes of many kinds, as well as giraffes and elephants."

"Will we get to see any predators?" you ask.

Endesha nods. "Of course. The park is full of lions, leopards, cheetahs, and crocodiles."

GO ON TO THE NEXT PAGE.

Both trips sound exciting!

WILL YOU . . .

. . . choose the Ngorongoro Conservation Area?
TURN TO PAGE 22.

. . . head to the Serengeti National Park?
TURN TO PAGE 94.

Maybe going south wasn't the greatest idea. The area appears deserted except for a huge termite mound, towering ten feet in the air.

Then Endesha stops the vehicle. "Look over there," he says, pointing. A rhinoceros is ambling slowly along near the termite mound. "That's a hook-lipped rhino," says Endesha. "We are very fortunate to see one. They're critically endangered."

"Look at those magnificent horns!" says one of the adults.

"The horns can grow to more than four feet long," says Endesha. "Sadly, they also make the rhinos a target for poachers. Some people prize rhino horns to make decorative objects, jewelry, or even medicine."

The rhino has turned his head toward the vehicle. "He's looking at us!" says another adult.

Endesha smiles. "I doubt it," he says. "Rhinos have very poor eyesight."

This is just the kind of thing you came here to see! And since it won't be able to see you, you climb out of the vehicle and head toward the rhino to get a better look.

GO ON TO THE NEXT PAGE.

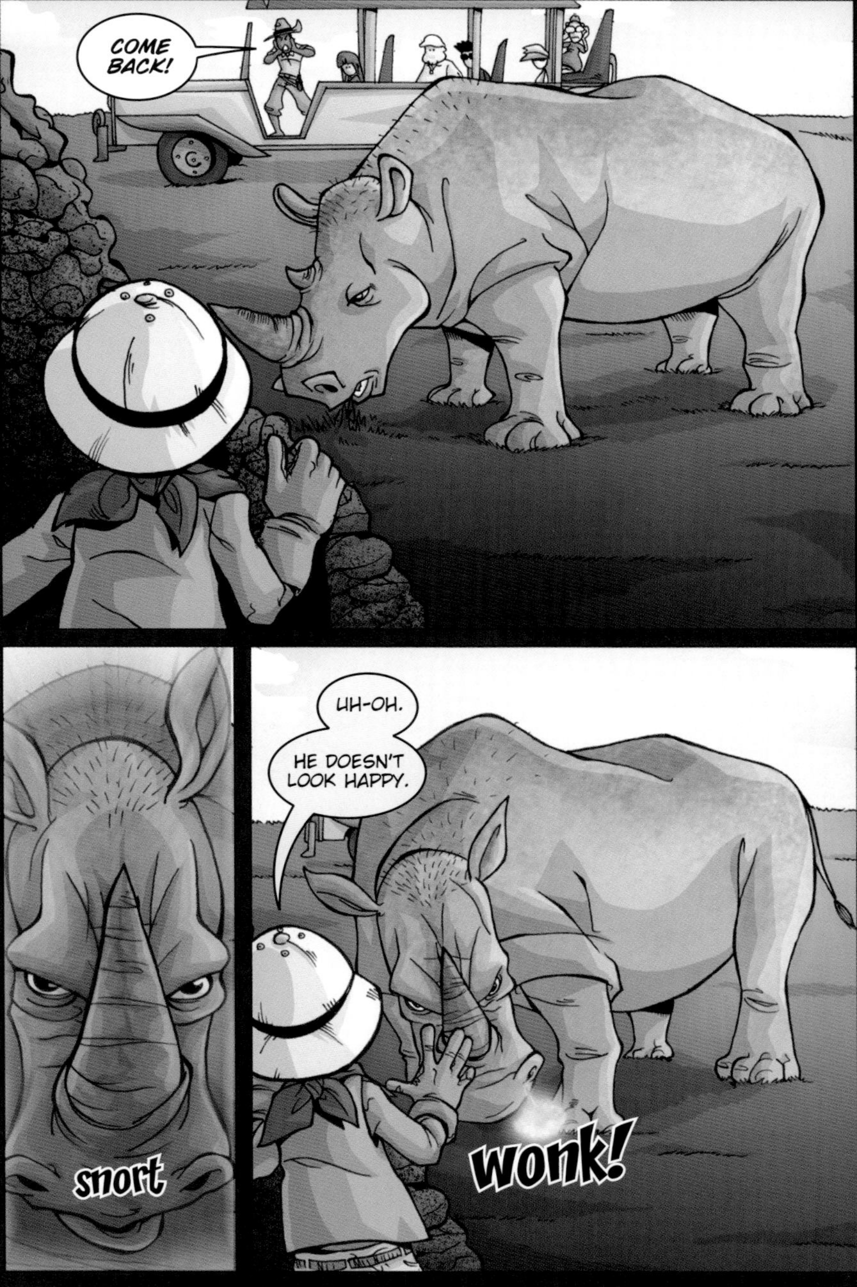
COME BACK!
UH-OH.
HE DOESN'T LOOK HAPPY.
snort
wonk!

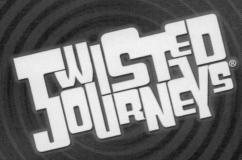

The rhino looks as if it's about to charge.

WILL YOU . . .

. . . drop to the ground?
TURN TO PAGE 109.

. . . make a lot of noise to frighten the rhino away?
TURN TO PAGE 45.

. . . run toward the safari vehicle?
TURN TO PAGE 74.

Lake
Victoria
Serengeti
TANZAN

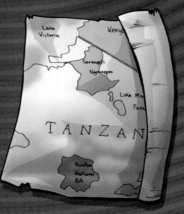

After an hour, the pilot gradually begins lowering the balloon toward an open area of grassland.

As the balloon descends, Endesha suddenly takes you by the shoulders and moves you to the other side of the basket. "Look that way," he says. "Not over here."

"Why?" you ask.

He hesitates but finally answers, "There's an elephant carcass over there with the tusks ripped out. It's a sight that no visitor to the park should ever have to see."

You get a sick feeling in your stomach. Suddenly you know exactly what those long, thin bundles were. "Endesha," you say slowly, "I think I saw a poachers' camp a while back."

Endesha turns to you quickly. "Really? Do you remember where it was? Can you point it out to me?"

You look down, ashamed. "No, I can't. I wasn't sure what it was. I should have said something then."

Endesha pats you on the shoulder. "Don't worry. Someday we'll find a way to stop them."

"I just wish I could have helped," you say.

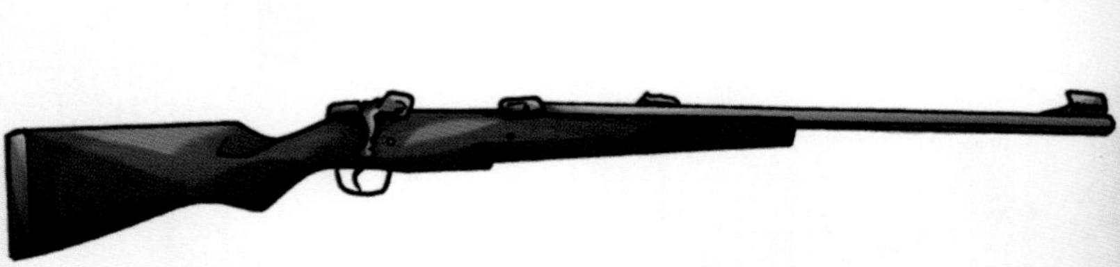

THE END

"Let me think about it for just a few more minutes," you say.

"That's fine," says Endesha. "I still need to get things ready, and you still need to get the rest of your gear. Let me know your decision when I get back."

The more you think about it, the more you realize that you don't want Endesha to babysit you. You figure there won't be any dangerous animals near the camp, so you can just go out and explore by yourself.

Taking another look at the map Endesha left, you notice a patch of woodlands nearby. That could be interesting!

You scribble a note. "I've gone out exploring. I'll be back for dinner!"

GO ON TO THE NEXT PAGE.

Endesha will be back in just a few minutes,
and you don't think he'll approve of your plan
to go out alone.

WILL YOU . . .

. . . head straight out while no one is looking?
TURN TO PAGE 97.

. . . detour back to your tent to pick up your water
bottle and risk being stopped by Endesha?
TURN TO PAGE 54.

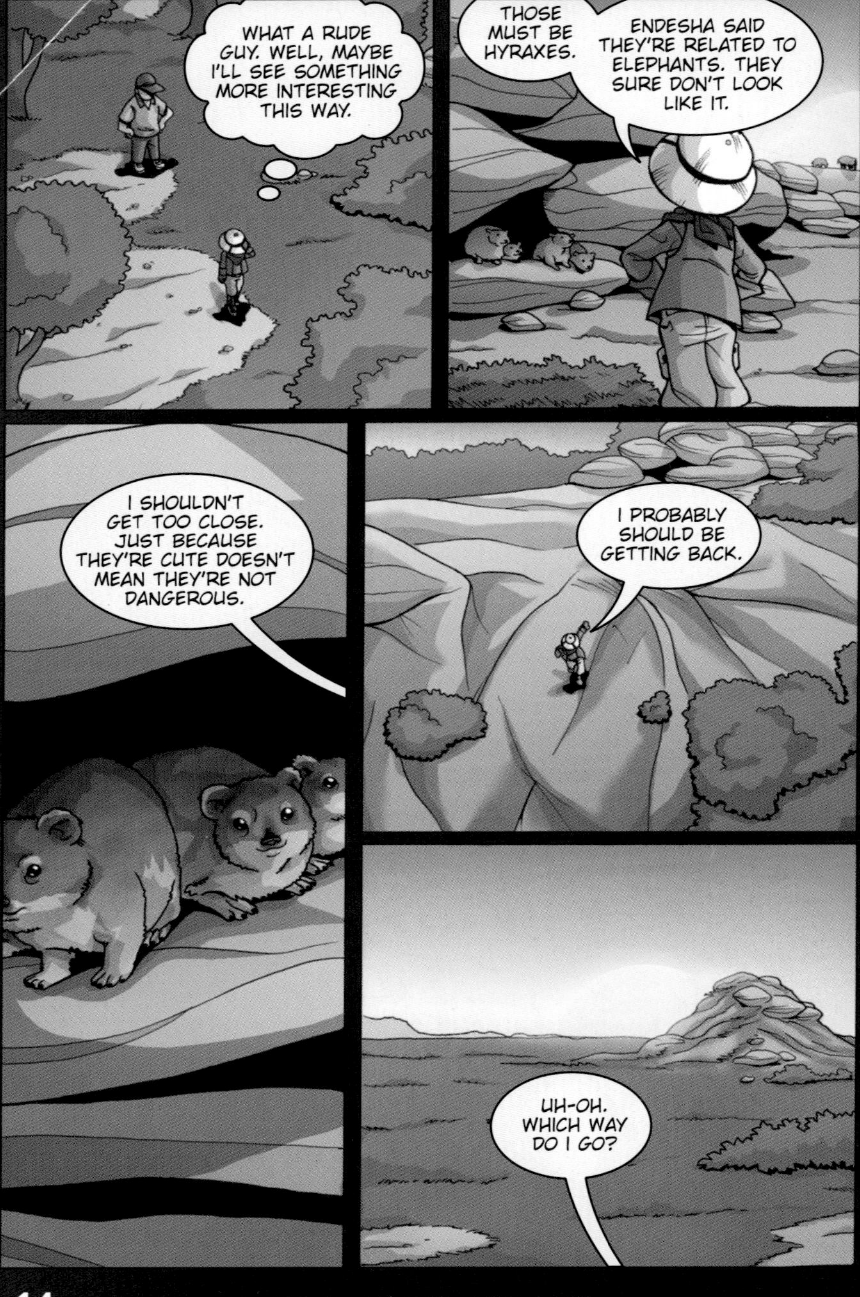
WHAT A RUDE GUY. WELL, MAYBE I'LL SEE SOMETHING MORE INTERESTING THIS WAY.
THOSE MUST BE HYRAXES.
ENDESHA SAID THEY'RE RELATED TO ELEPHANTS. THEY SURE DON'T LOOK LIKE IT.
I SHOULDN'T GET TOO CLOSE. JUST BECAUSE THEY'RE CUTE DOESN'T MEAN THEY'RE NOT DANGEROUS.
I PROBABLY SHOULD BE GETTING BACK.
UH-OH. WHICH WAY DO I GO?

GO ON TO THE NEXT PAGE.

You look around. In every direction you see the exact same thing: grasslands and those small rocky hills Endesha calls kopjes. Picking a direction at random, you set out, hoping to see a familiar landmark.

Suddenly you hear a familiar sound. It sounds like barking. You turn in the direction of the sound and see a pack of dogs bounding up toward you. They must be rescue dogs that Endesha sent to find you!

You squat down and hold out your hand to the nearest dog. "Here, boy!" That's when he bares his teeth, and you notice he's not wearing a collar.

GO ON TO THE NEXT PAGE.

Dogs are very good at hunting in packs. Even as you back away from the slavering jaws of the dog in front of you, two more have circled around behind you. In desperation, you swing your water bottle at one of them. He clamps onto your arm with teeth like knives.

One of the other dogs rushes at your legs. Trying to avoid another painful bite, you trip over your own feet and fall to the ground. Looking up, you see that you are surrounded by gleaming eyes and shining teeth. Lots and lots of teeth.

Wild dogs are successful in 70 percent of their hunts, even with experienced prey—which you are not.

THE END

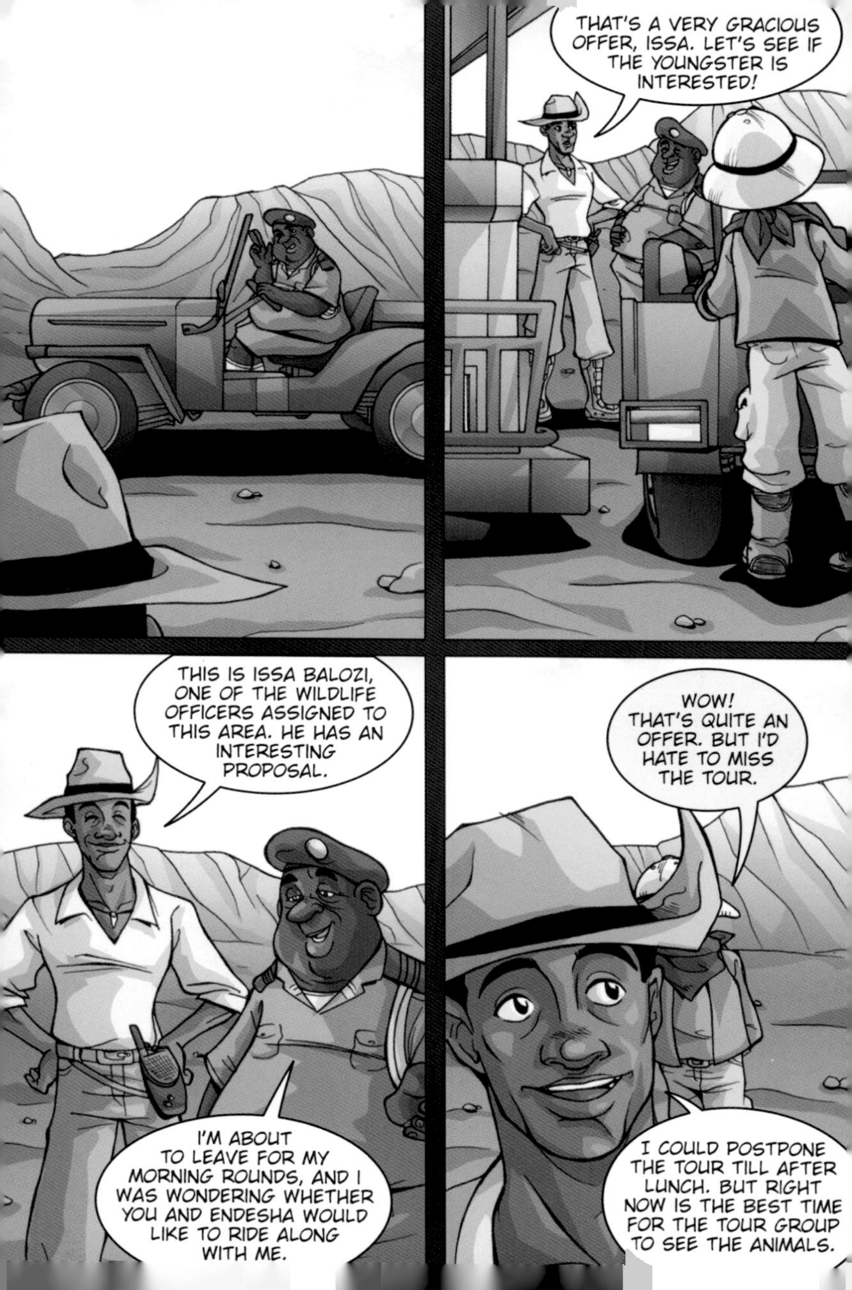
THAT'S A VERY GRACIOUS OFFER, ISSA. LET'S SEE IF THE YOUNGSTER IS INTERESTED!
THIS IS ISSA BALOZI, ONE OF THE WILDLIFE OFFICERS ASSIGNED TO THIS AREA. HE HAS AN INTERESTING PROPOSAL.
I'M ABOUT TO LEAVE FOR MY MORNING ROUNDS, AND I WAS WONDERING WHETHER YOU AND ENDESHA WOULD LIKE TO RIDE ALONG WITH ME.
WOW! THAT'S QUITE AN OFFER. BUT I'D HATE TO MISS THE TOUR.
I COULD POSTPONE THE TOUR TILL AFTER LUNCH. BUT RIGHT NOW IS THE BEST TIME FOR THE TOUR GROUP TO SEE THE ANIMALS.

TWISTED JOURNEYS®

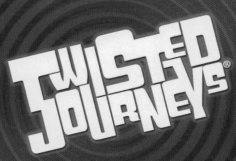

Both activities sound interesting!

WILL YOU . . .

. . . ride along with the wildlife officer?
TURN TO PAGE 106.

. . . go with the tour group?
TURN TO PAGE 100.

Lake
Victoria
TANZAN

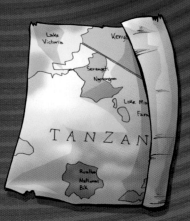

You walk down to the lake. Laura is hunched over her game as usual.

"Hey," you say. "Why'd you come down here?"

She doesn't look up. "My parents aren't here. That's why."

"It's a good thing there aren't any crocodiles or hippos here now," you say. "You'd give them a stomachache."

"Brat," she says.

The lake water looks clear and cool. Taking off your shoes and socks, you wade in.

After splashing around awhile, you look for stones to skip across the water, but you don't see any good ones. Looking down, you notice some grassy clumps floating nearby. They don't skip well, but they squish nicely when you throw them against a rock. You're tempted to throw one at Laura . . . but you decide you'd better not.

Suddenly you hear Endesha shouting. "Get back up here right now and WASH YOUR HANDS!"

GO ON TO THE NEXT PAGE.

You head back up to the rest area. Endesha points to the washroom. "Twice! And use lots of soap!" You obey hastily.

When you come out, you ask, "Why all the washing, Endesha?"

"Do you know what you were throwing?"

"Uh . . . grass? And mud?"

Endesha allows himself to smile. "No, my young friend. Hippopotamus poop!"

"Ewww!"

Going back to the lake, you start putting on your shoes and socks when you feel a sharp pain in your left foot. You pull off your shoe and look inside. A scorpion is staring back at you!

"I've been stung by a scorpion!" you scream. "I'm gonna die!"

Endesha comes running and looks in your shoe. "Are you allergic to bee stings?" he asks.

"No."

"Then relax. It's a common red claw scorpion. You're lucky—its sting isn't serious. But from now on, remember to shake out your shoes before you put them on!"

It's a lesson you'll keep in mind for the rest of your safari.

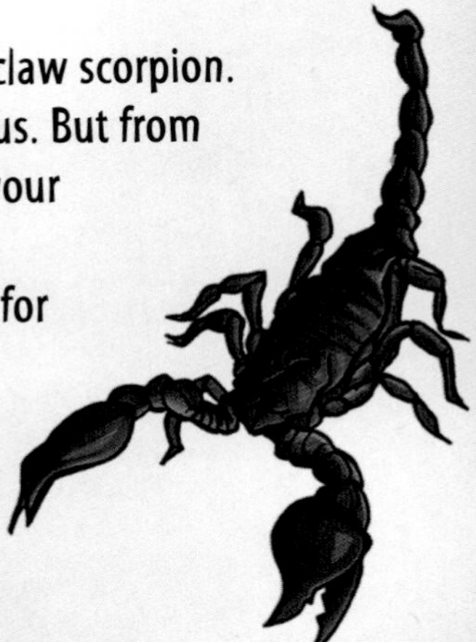

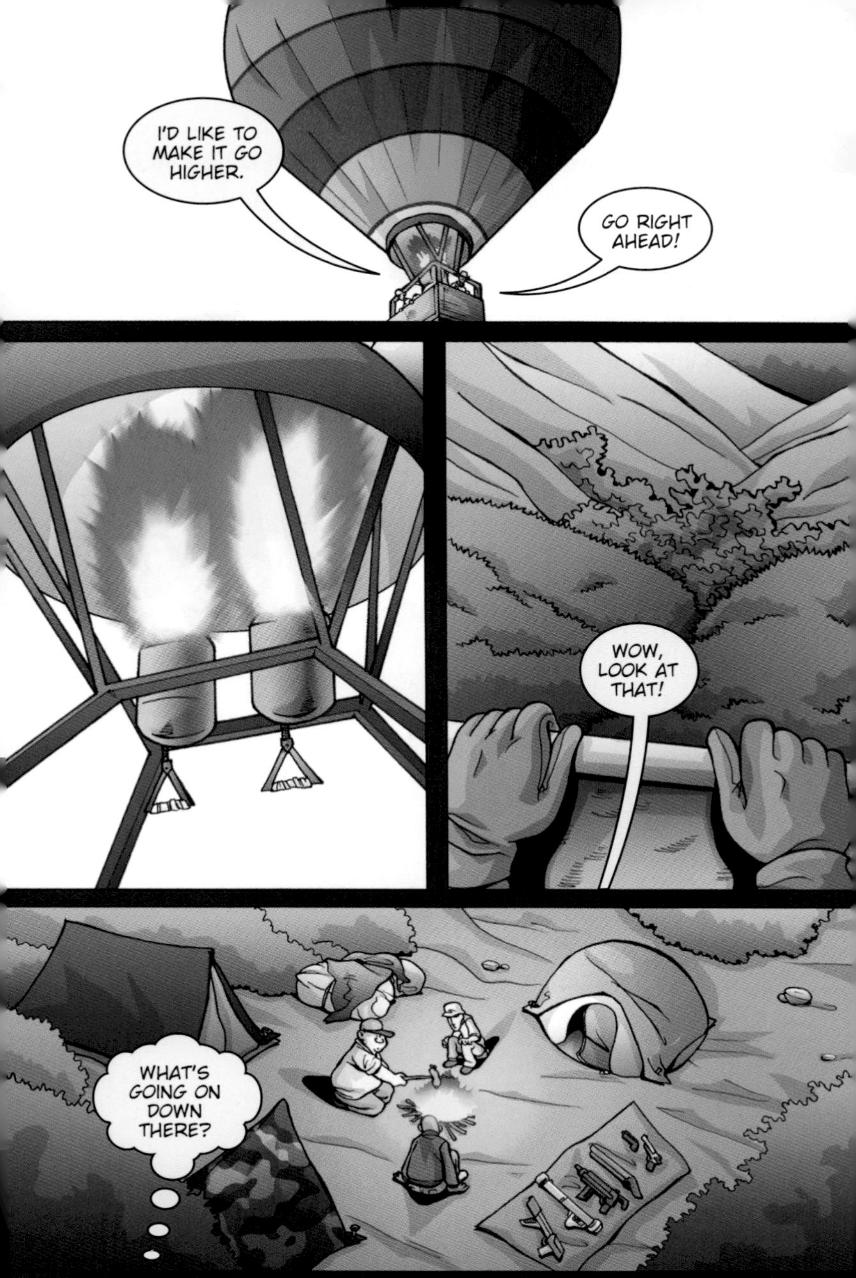
I'D LIKE TO MAKE IT GO HIGHER.
GO RIGHT AHEAD!
WOW, LOOK AT THAT!
WHAT'S GOING ON DOWN THERE?

TURN TO PAGE 34.

"That's a great choice," says Endesha. "You won't be disappointed."

After dinner, you spend the evening packing. You think you'll be too excited to sleep, but you're so tired that you fall asleep as soon as your head hits the pillow.

The next morning, you have breakfast with the rest of your family, then wave good-bye to them cheerfully. Then you run eagerly toward the safari vehicle preparing to leave for the Ngorongoro Conservation Area.

GO ON TO THE NEXT PAGE.

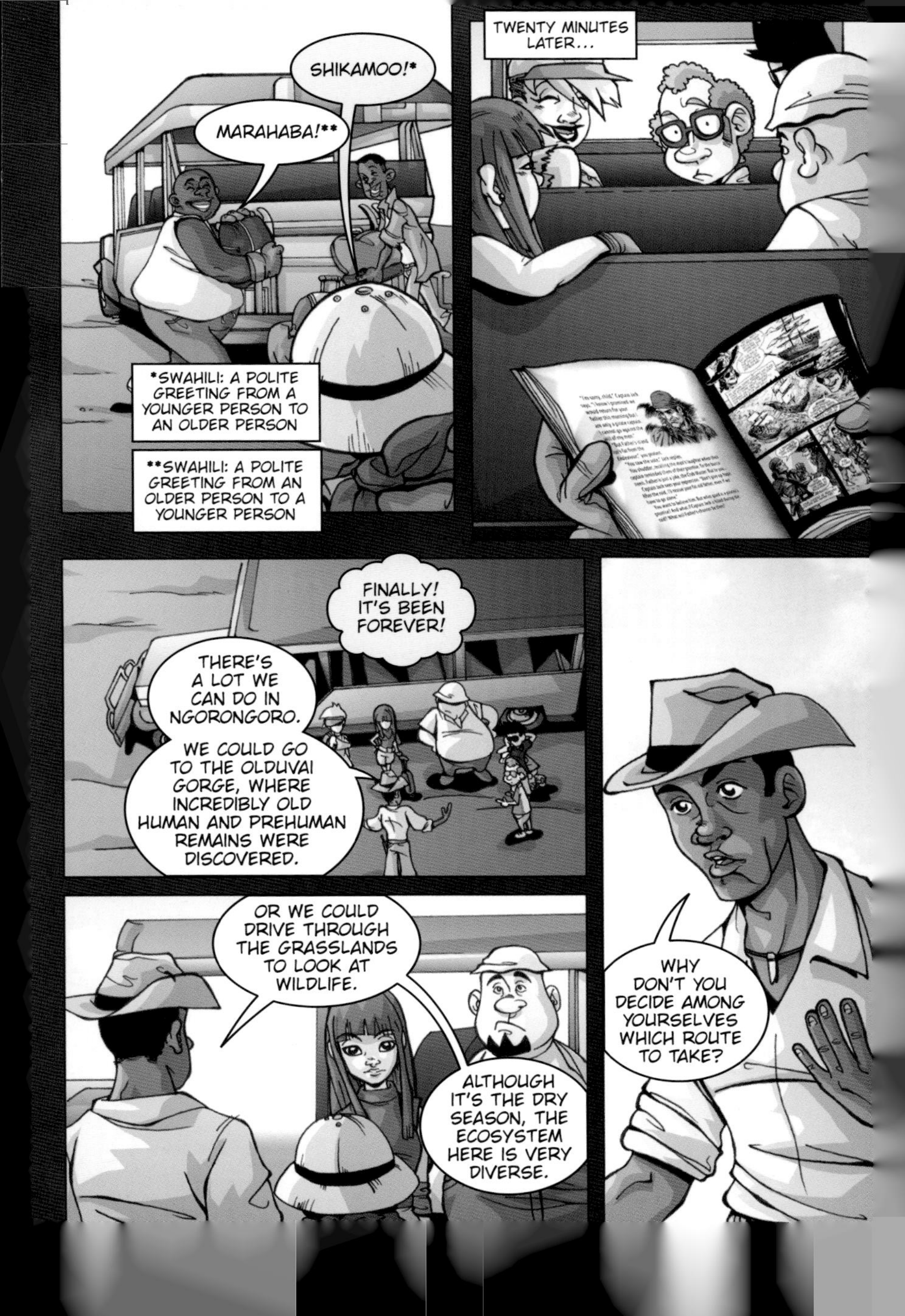
SHIKAMOO!*
MARAHABA!**
*SWAHILI: A POLITE GREETING FROM A YOUNGER PERSON TO AN OLDER PERSON
**SWAHILI: A POLITE GREETING FROM AN OLDER PERSON TO A YOUNGER PERSON
TWENTY MINUTES LATER...
FINALLY! IT'S BEEN FOREVER!
THERE'S A LOT WE CAN DO IN NGORONGORO.
WE COULD GO TO THE OLDUVAI GORGE, WHERE INCREDIBLY OLD HUMAN AND PREHUMAN REMAINS WERE DISCOVERED.
OR WE COULD DRIVE THROUGH THE GRASSLANDS TO LOOK AT WILDLIFE.
ALTHOUGH IT'S THE DRY SEASON, THE ECOSYSTEM HERE IS VERY DIVERSE.
WHY DON'T YOU DECIDE AMONG YOURSELVES WHICH ROUTE TO TAKE?

TWISTED JOURNEYS®

WILL YOU . . .

. . . suggest a visit the Olduvai Gorge?
TURN TO PAGE 64.

. . . convince the others to take a ride through the grasslands in search of wildlife?
TURN TO PAGE 41.

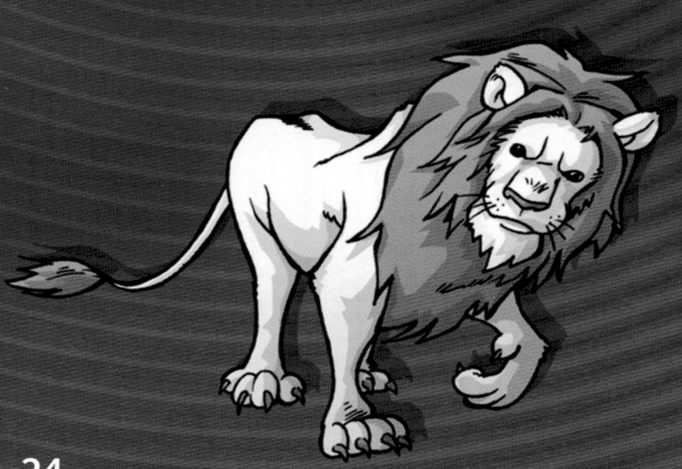

You duck back through the curtain into the stall and run into the main road. You spot a group of police officers nearby.

"Ma'am!" you call to the nearest one as you approach. "That shop—there's a back room where they sell things made of ivory."

She nods. "Are there customers in there right now?"

"Yes."

She beckons to the other police officers. "We have a chance to catch them in the act," she tells them. "Let's go!"

A few minutes later, you see the police coming out of the stall, leading the shopkeeper and the parents in handcuffs, the kids trailing behind. The policewoman comes over and puts her hand on your shoulder. "You did a good deed today," she says. "The more of these shops we shut down, the more elephants we save."

"I'm glad I could help," you say, and you mean every word.

THE END

"They're killing wild animals in a protected area," you say. "Arrest them!"

"I appreciate your zeal," Mr. Balozi responds. "But this man and his son are poor farmers who hunt in the park to provide meat for their family. They usually kill only one animal at a time. With millions of wildebeest roaming the park, the loss of a few thousand to hungry people is not our most pressing concern."

Mr. Balozi looks at the two hunters carefully and says, "Since they haven't killed any animals today, I would prefer not to arrest them. My time would be better spent pursuing the professional poachers, the ones who provide merchandise to a multimillion-dollar black market, the ones who use modern weaponry to kill thousands of animals—and anyone else who gets in their way."

You come away with a new understanding . . . and a new compassion as well.

THE END

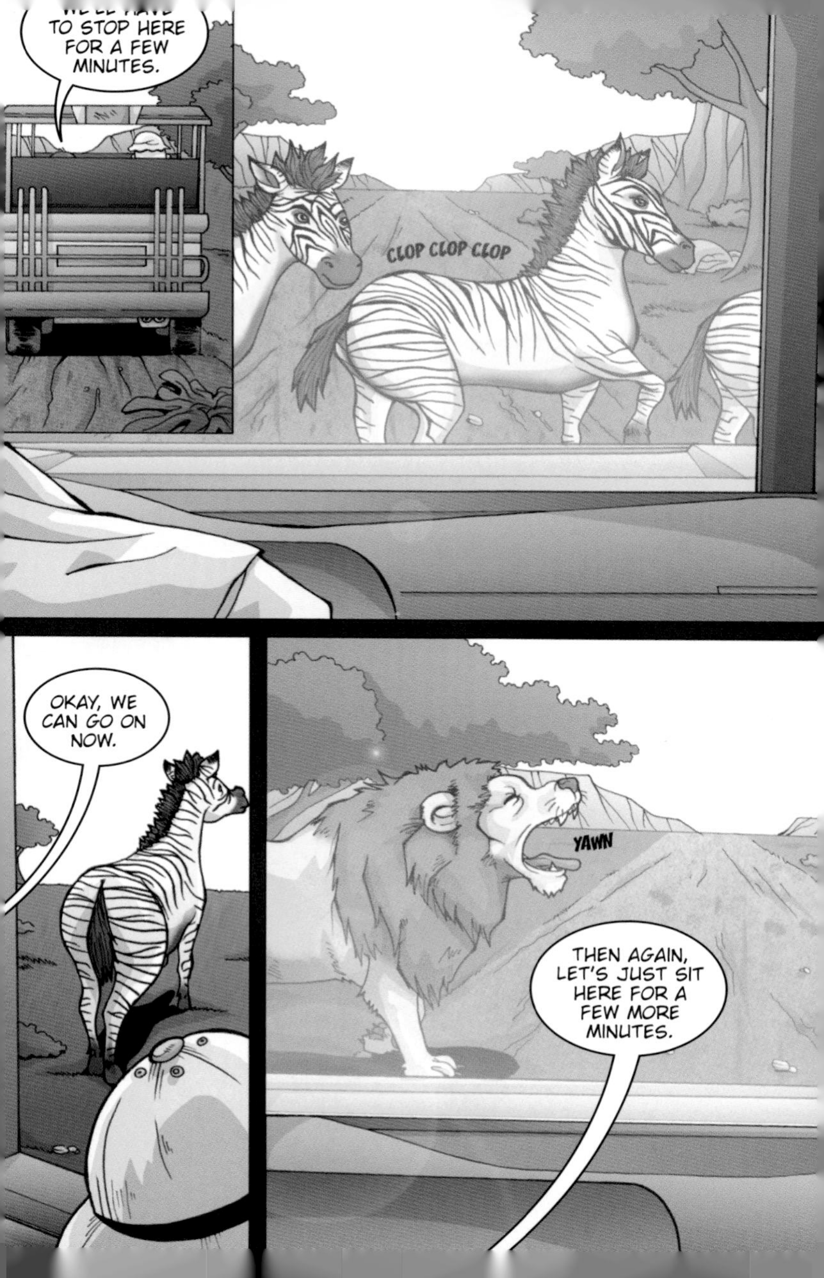
TO STOP HERE FOR A FEW MINUTES.
CLOP CLOP CLOP
OKAY, WE CAN GO ON NOW.
YAWN
THEN AGAIN, LET'S JUST SIT HERE FOR A FEW MORE MINUTES.

Everyone is silent as the lion strolls alongside the vehicle. He's almost near enough to reach out and touch. You can see his thick, deep gold fur up close. You can even spot bits of dirt and leaves clinging to him here and there from his most recent nap.

Eventually the lion wanders away. You all look at one another for a moment. No one wants to speak and break the spell. Finally, you say what everyone has been thinking: "Wow."

Endesha grins. "You got that right!" He starts up the engine, and the vehicle travels down the road a few miles before coming to a fork.

"We can go either north or south here," says Endesha. "We've had reports of large groups of herd animals congregating in the north. We can investigate them further. Or we head to the open spaces to the south, where we might see some more solitary wildlife."

GO ON TO THE NEXT PAGE.

The group looks to you to make a choice.

WILL YOU . . .

. . . go north for the large herds?
TURN TO PAGE 67.

. . . go south in search of solitary animals?
TURN TO PAGE 8.

A good distance from the vehicle, you and the adults are wandering aimlessly, but that's okay with you. After riding for so long, it feels good to walk around.

One of them stops suddenly and points. "Hey, who's that?"

There's a native walking along a short distance away with a large backpack on his back. When he sees the group, he smiles, gives a friendly wave, and starts walking toward you.

GO ON TO THE NEXT PAGE.

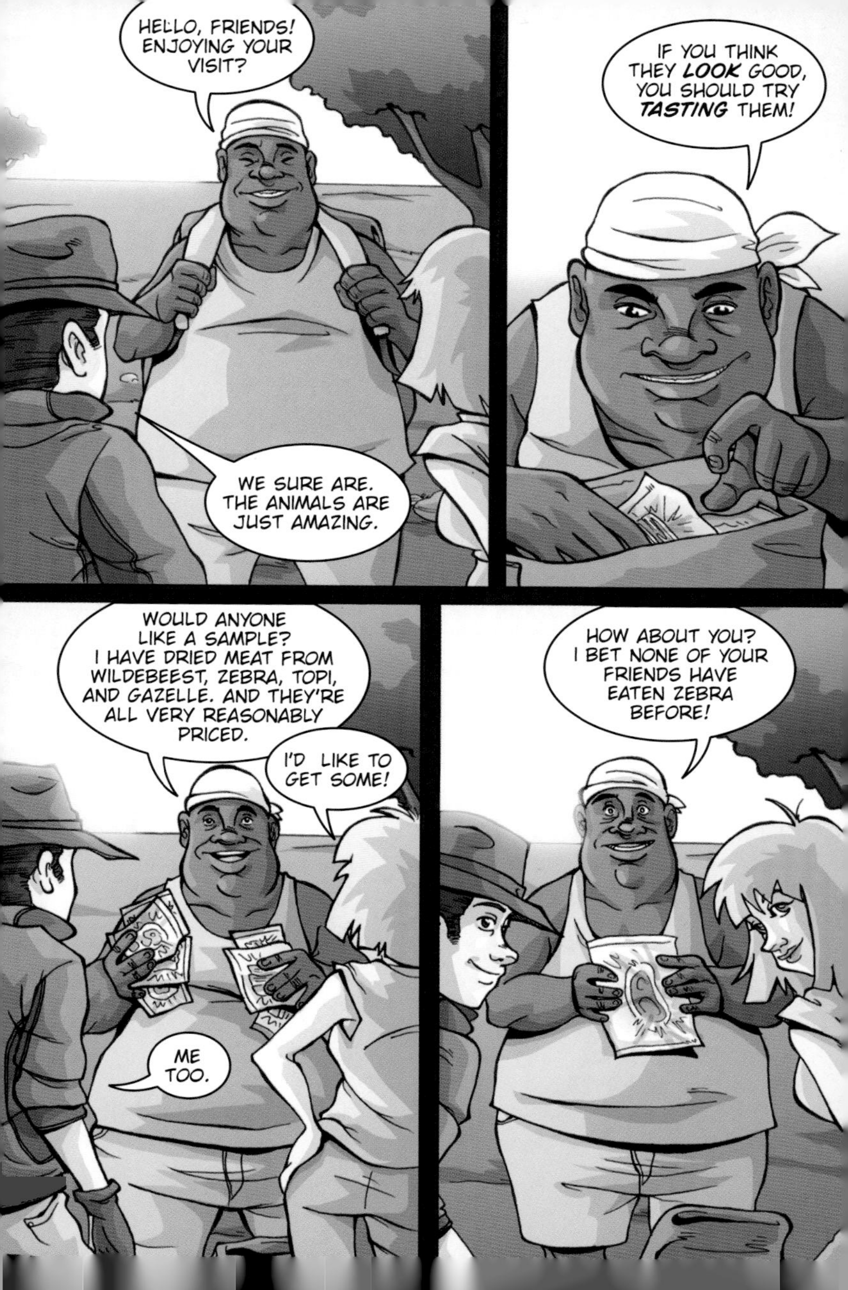
HELLO, FRIENDS! ENJOYING YOUR VISIT?
WE SURE ARE. THE ANIMALS ARE JUST AMAZING.
IF YOU THINK THEY **LOOK** GOOD, YOU SHOULD TRY ***TASTING*** THEM!
WOULD ANYONE LIKE A SAMPLE? I HAVE DRIED MEAT FROM WILDEBEEST, ZEBRA, TOPI, AND GAZELLE. AND THEY'RE ALL VERY REASONABLY PRICED.
I'D LIKE TO GET SOME!
ME TOO.
HOW ABOUT YOU? I BET NONE OF YOUR FRIENDS HAVE EATEN ZEBRA BEFORE!

TWISTED JOURNEYS®

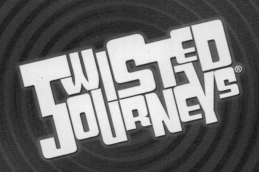

Wouldn't it be great to tell your friends back home that you've not only *seen* wild animals, but you've *eaten* them? On the other hand, you know it's illegal.

WILL YOU . . .

. . . buy some wild animal meat?
TURN TO PAGE 63.

. . . turn down the dealer's offer?
TURN TO PAGE 75.

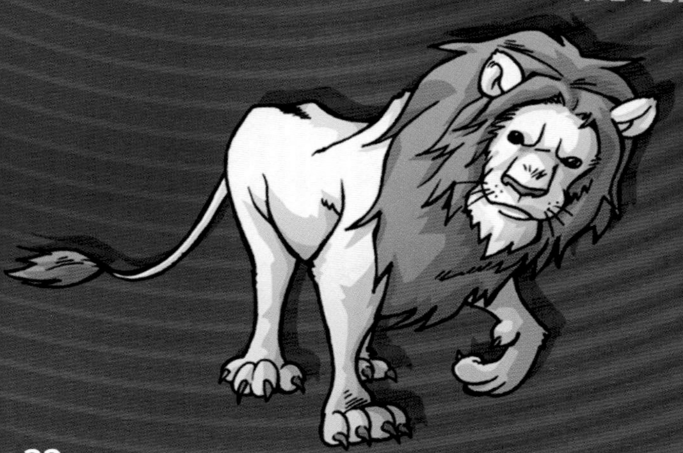

"Well, they haven't actually killed anything yet," you say. "And the kid . . . he's the same age as me. I'd hate to see him go to jail."

Mr. Balozi nods his agreement. "They're not greedy," he says. "They're just hungry." He looks very serious. "If they had been carrying rifles instead of bows and arrows, I would have sent a party of rangers after them later.

"I don't want to put people like them behind bars. I need to find out how their needs can be met so they don't have to hunt in the park for food." He has a long conversation with the man in Swahili. You can't tell what they're saying, but they're obviously relieved not to be arrested. As they turn to leave, you wave good-bye to the boy, and he waves back.

Before you came to Africa, you thought you'd just be looking at wild animals. Now you realize that the animals are part of a whole ecosystem that includes people and their needs as well.

THE END

TWISTED JOURNEYS®

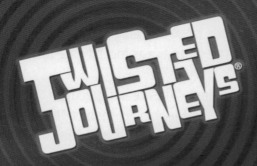

You don't want to be nosy, but you're curious about what those people are up to.

WILL YOU . . .

. . . keep it to yourself, since it's none of your business?

TURN TO PAGE 11.

. . . point them out to Endesha and the pilot?

TURN TO PAGE 103.

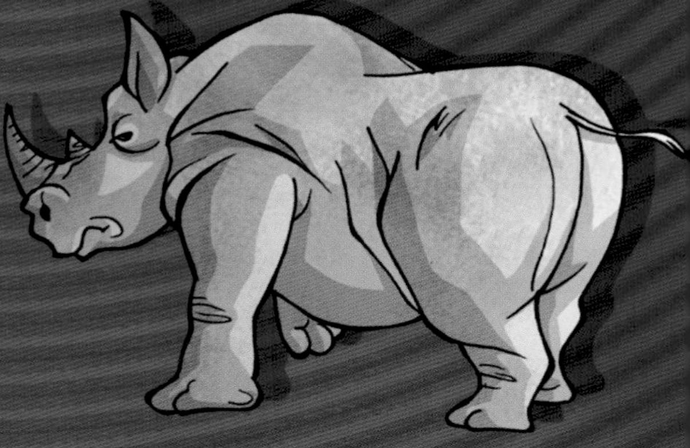

Just as you begin to step carefully away from the edge, you hear a sound like an explosion deep inside the volcano. A foul-smelling, incredibly hot cloud of ash blasts upward from the crater. You try to hold your breath, but you can't help breathing some of it in. You fall to the ground, gasping to get fresh air into your scorched lungs. In the background, you can hear Endesha calling on the radio for an emergency helicopter.

You awake to find yourself in the hospital, where a doctor tells you that you've contracted a disease called pneumonoultramicroscopicsilicovolcanoconiosis from breathing in the volcanic ash. You may need treatment for the rest of your life, but at least you've been diagnosed with a disease that is the longest word in the English language!

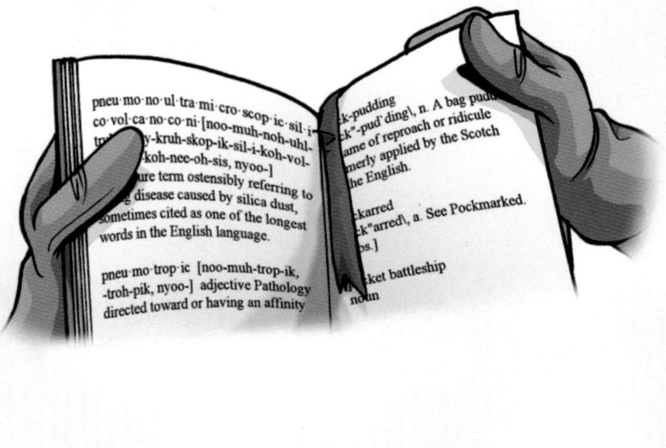
pneu·mo·no·ul·tra·mi·cro·scop·ic·sil·i·
co·vol·ca·no·co·ni·[noo-muh-noh-uhl-
-kruh-skop-ik-sil-i-koh-vol-
koh-nee-oh-sis, nyoo-]
term ostensibly referring to
disease caused by silica dust,
sometimes cited as one of the longest
words in the English language.
pneu·mo·trop·ic [noo-muh-trop-ik,
-troh-pik, nyoo-] adjective Pathology
directed toward or having an affinity
k-pudding
k"-pud'ding\, n. A bag pud
ame of reproach or ridicule
merly applied by the Scotch
he English.
kmarred
k"arred\, a. See Pockmarked.
ket battleship
noun

THE END

"This park is so huge," you say, "that there's plenty to do right here."

Endesha smiles. "I agree with you!" he says. "Here are some places that you might go." He takes out a map of the park and puts his finger on a spot near the bottom. "Here's where we are now, in the grasslands area. There are a lot of animals to see here. We could ride out and explore the grasslands in-depth.

"If you'd like to see a very different ecosystem, the thorn tree woodlands in the north would be just the thing. We can take a small plane to get there."

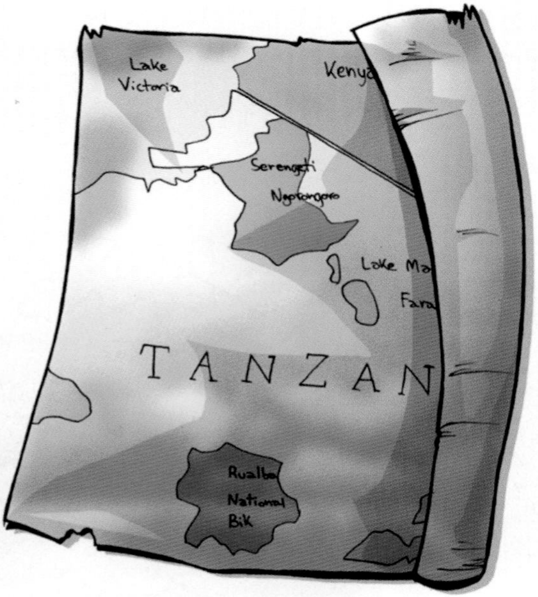
Lake Victoria
Kenya
Serengeti
Lake Ma
Fara
TANZAN
Rualba National Bik

GO ON TO THE NEXT PAGE.

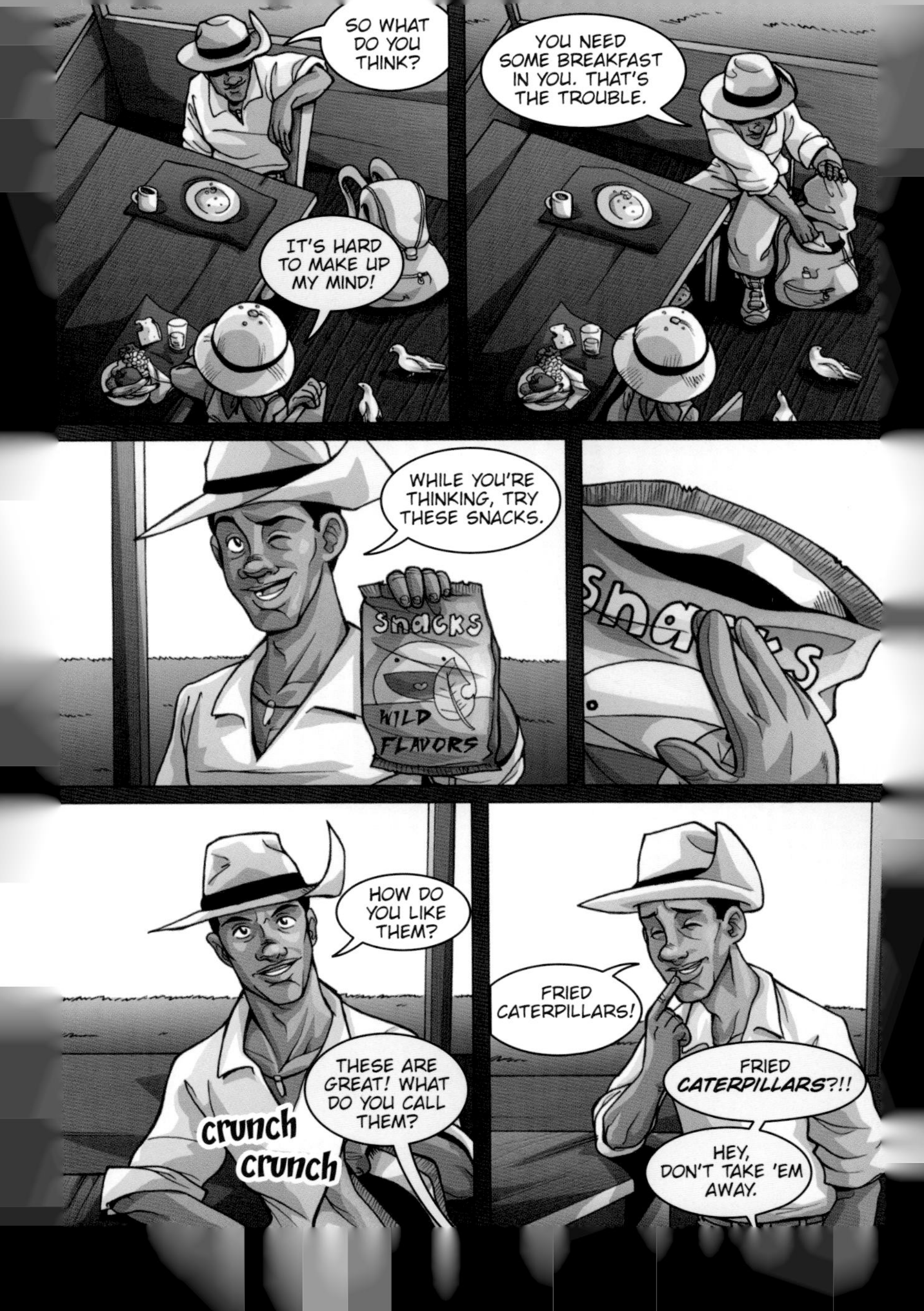
SO WHAT DO YOU THINK?
IT'S HARD TO MAKE UP MY MIND!
YOU NEED SOME BREAKFAST IN YOU. THAT'S THE TROUBLE.
WHILE YOU'RE THINKING, TRY THESE SNACKS.
SNACKS
WILD FLAVORS
HOW DO YOU LIKE THEM?
crunch
crunch
THESE ARE GREAT! WHAT DO YOU CALL THEM?
FRIED CATERPILLARS!
FRIED CATERPILLARS?!!
HEY, DON'T TAKE 'EM AWAY.

TWISTED JOURNEYS®

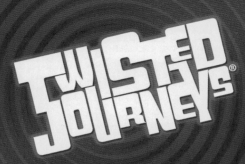

Now that you've had some brain food,
it's time to make your choice!

WILL YOU . . .

. . . take a plane ride to the thorn tree woodlands?
TURN TO PAGE 86.

. . . stall for time so you can plan an adventure all by yourself?
TURN TO PAGE 12.

. . . explore the grasslands?
TURN TO PAGE 17.

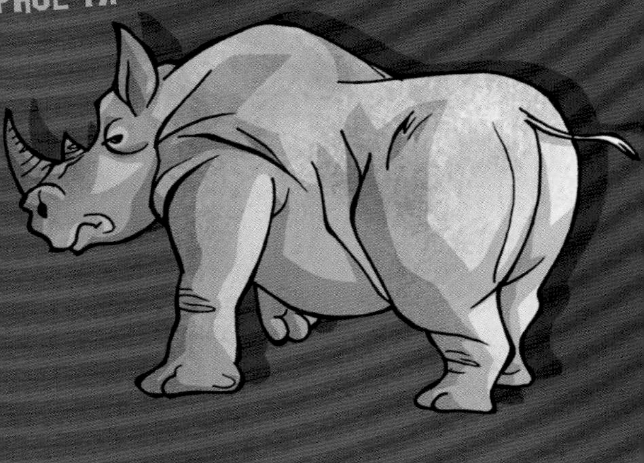

Endesha drops you off at the market, pointing out a place to meet him in an hour. For the first time since you got to Africa, you can wander where you like. You practice your polite greeting on the shopkeepers, who never fail to give you a friendly response.

Going into a nice-looking shop, you notice a family with two kids talking with the shopkeeper. As you look at inexpensive souvenirs made of wood and plastic, you overhear the mother saying quietly, "We're looking for something a little more . . . authentic."

The shopkeeper nods and beckons them to follow him behind a curtain hanging at the back of the stall. Maybe there's something more interesting back there! You follow along, hoping no one notices.

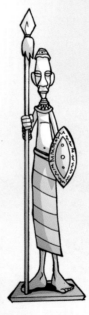

The back area is fully enclosed, and you realize that figurines back here aren't plastic. They're . . .

"Real elephant ivory," the father says approvingly. "Now that's what we're looking for."

GO ON TO THE NEXT PAGE.

TWISTED JOURNEYS®

You know that what the shopkeeper's doing is illegal.

WILL YOU . . .

. . . slip out and inform the authorities?
TURN TO PAGE 25.

. . . stay where you are and try not to be noticed?
TURN TO PAGE 81.

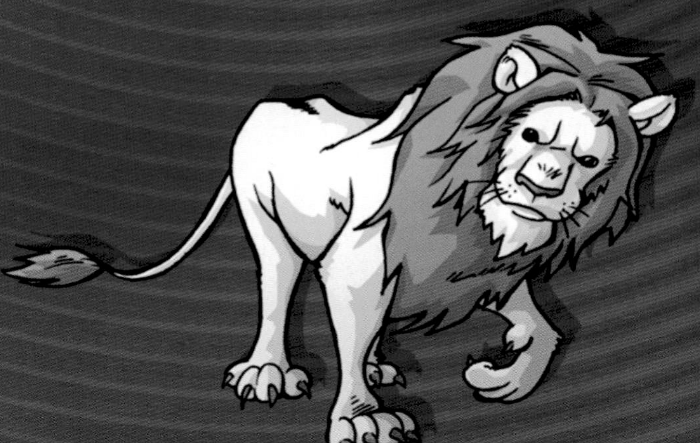

As you're riding through the grasslands, Endesha pulls the vehicle off the road and stops next to a rock formation. Then he turns to face the tour group. "Folks, this type of small rocky hill is called a kopje. This one has a watering hole on the far side, and we often see wildlife here. Let's all get out very quietly and take a look!"

You follow Endesha around the rocks. The watering hole looks deserted.

But wait—something big and dark is moving under an overhanging ledge of rock. You can't quite make out what it is . . .

Suddenly one of the adults in the group freaks out. "Run!" he yells. "Back to the vehicle! Quick!"

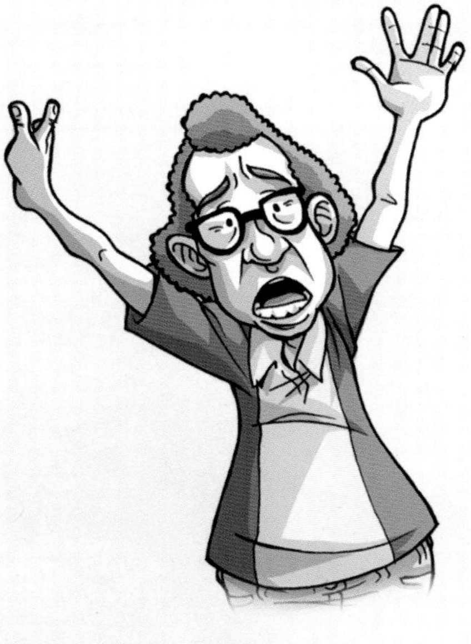

GO ON TO THE NEXT PAGE.

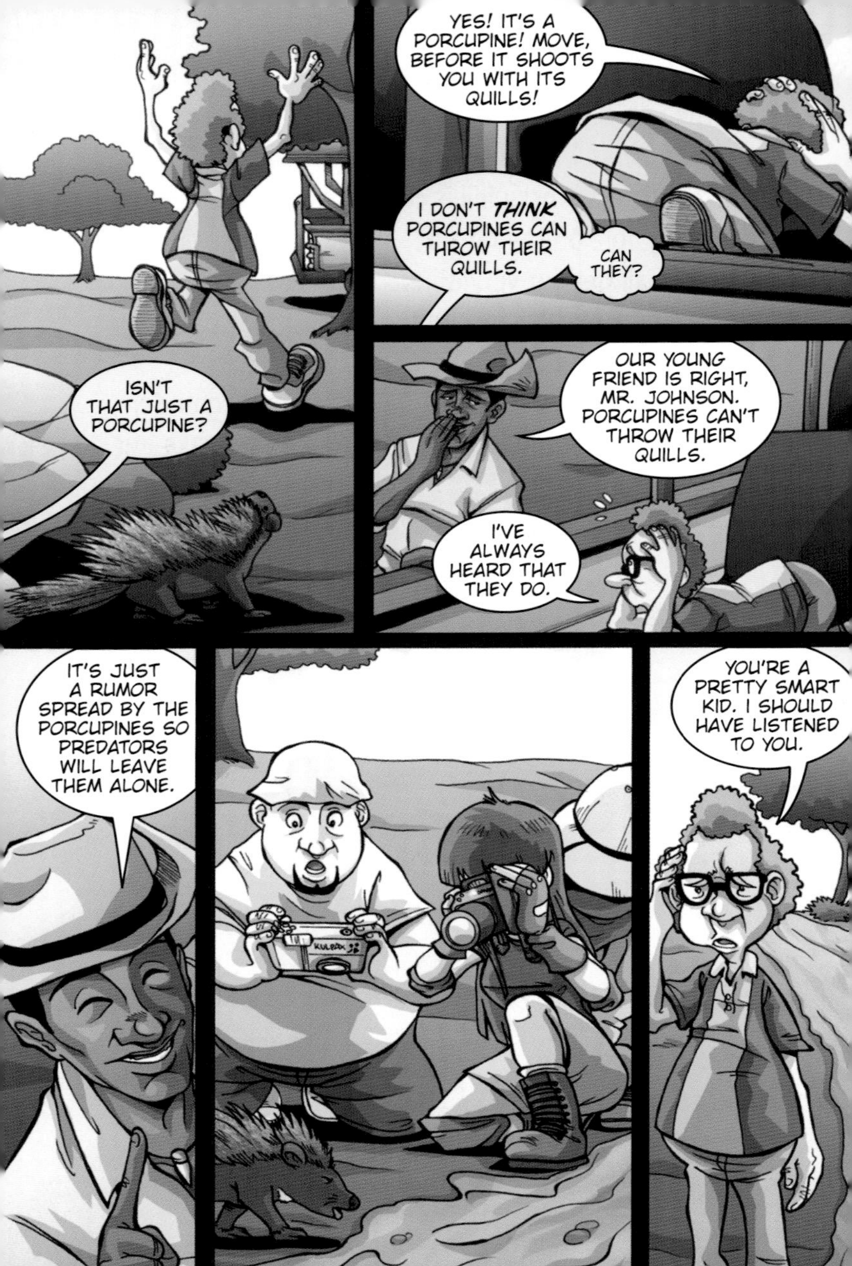
ISN'T THAT JUST A PORCUPINE?
YES! IT'S A PORCUPINE! MOVE, BEFORE IT SHOOTS YOU WITH ITS QUILLS!
I DON'T THINK PORCUPINES CAN THROW THEIR QUILLS.
CAN THEY?
OUR YOUNG FRIEND IS RIGHT, MR. JOHNSON. PORCUPINES CAN'T THROW THEIR QUILLS.
I'VE ALWAYS HEARD THAT THEY DO.
IT'S JUST A RUMOR SPREAD BY THE PORCUPINES SO PREDATORS WILL LEAVE THEM ALONE.
YOU'RE A PRETTY SMART KID. I SHOULD HAVE LISTENED TO YOU.

You all get back into the vehicle. You'll never admit that you weren't really sure about porcupines not throwing their quills.

A short time later, the vehicle pulls over to the side of the road again. "We're going to have some tea," says Endesha, "and then we can talk about where to explore next. I suggest that we either drive to the foot of Mount Lengai and hike up to the volcanic crater or that we continue onto the plain to look for more animals."

Mr. Johnson turns to you. "What do you recommend?"

GO ON TO THE NEXT PAGE.

TWISTED JOURNEYS®

It's up to you!

WILL YOU . . .

. . . climb up the volcano and get a look inside the crater?

TURN TO PAGE 90.

. . . set out in search of more wildlife?

TURN TO PAGE 70.

Lake Victoria
Kenya
Serengeti
TANZAN

You jump up and down, yelling at the top of your lungs. "Go away! Leave me alone!"

Your shouts accomplish two things: you convince the rhino you're a threat, and you help him find you despite his poor eyesight.

You learn from personal experience that the rhino's horn is exactly as sharp as it looks.

THE END

You stare at the lion, who stares calmly back at you. Even though female lions do most of the hunting, you know that a male lion can still be dangerous. He doesn't seem to be looking for food, but you don't want him to interrupt his stroll for a snack.

You think you hear a hissing sound nearby. You look around for a snake, but don't see one. Then you hear the sound again, just loud enough to make it out. It's a human voice!

"Psst! This way!"

GO ON TO THE NEXT PAGE.

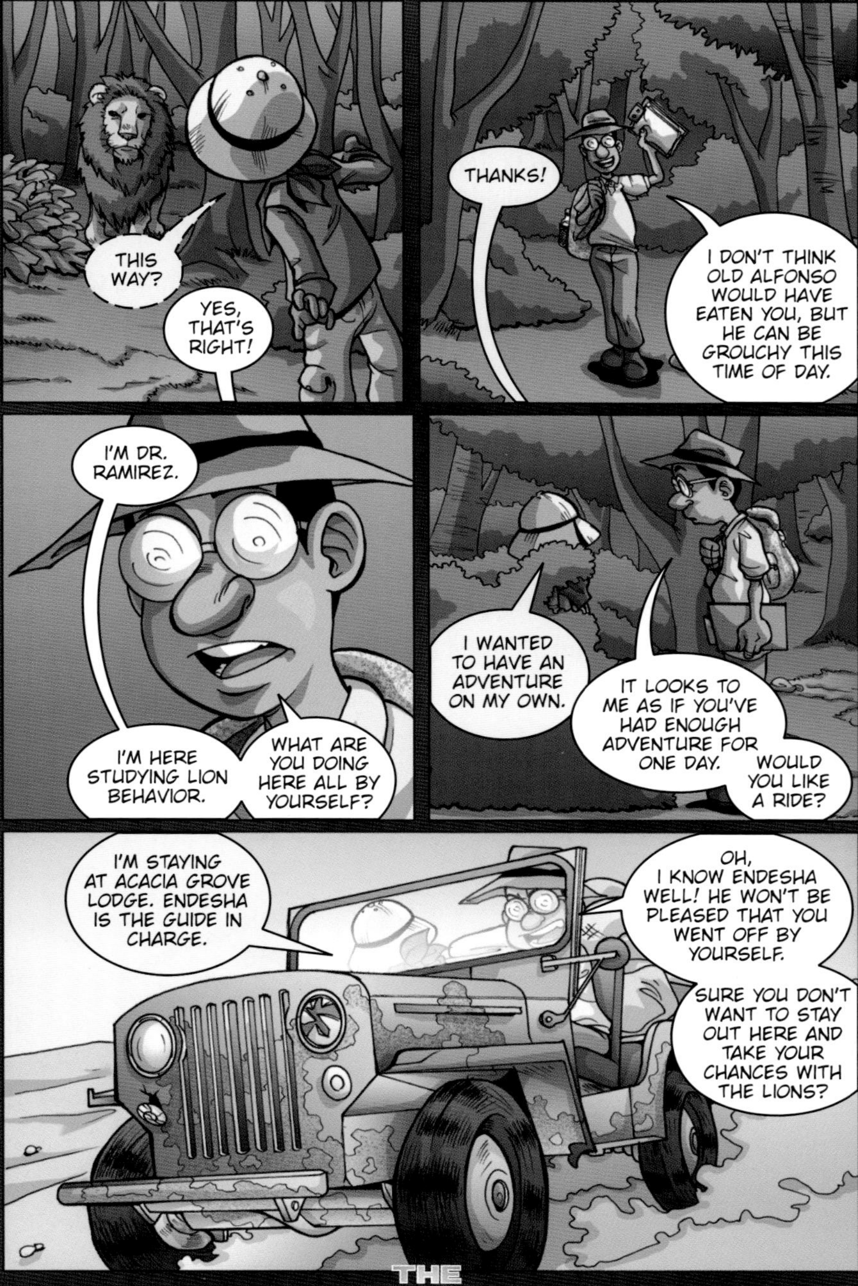
THIS WAY?
YES, THAT'S RIGHT!
THANKS!
I DON'T THINK OLD ALFONSO WOULD HAVE EATEN YOU, BUT HE CAN BE GROUCHY THIS TIME OF DAY.
I'M DR. RAMIREZ.
I'M HERE STUDYING LION BEHAVIOR.
WHAT ARE YOU DOING HERE ALL BY YOURSELF?
I WANTED TO HAVE AN ADVENTURE ON MY OWN.
IT LOOKS TO ME AS IF YOU'VE HAD ENOUGH ADVENTURE FOR ONE DAY.
WOULD YOU LIKE A RIDE?
I'M STAYING AT ACACIA GROVE LODGE. ENDESHA IS THE GUIDE IN CHARGE.
OH, I KNOW ENDESHA WELL! HE WON'T BE PLEASED THAT YOU WENT OFF BY YOURSELF.
SURE YOU DON'T WANT TO STAY OUT HERE AND TAKE YOUR CHANCES WITH THE LIONS?

THE END

After a short drive, you approach a group of vultures picking at an animal carcass. As Mr. Balozi approaches, the vultures hop away, flapping their wings.

"This animal was killed by a lion," he reports. "Not by poachers."

He looks around and sees a couple of natives coming to check out the animal kill. "Wait here," he says. He sets off at a trot and returns moments later escorting a man and a boy about your age. The man is wearing jeans with a belt, from which coiled wires are hanging, but no shirt or shoes. The boy, who is also barefoot, is wearing a faded T-shirt and shorts. They are both very thin. Mr. Balozi is holding their bows and arrows.

"Look," he says. "They were carrying poaching gear. What do you think I should do with them?"

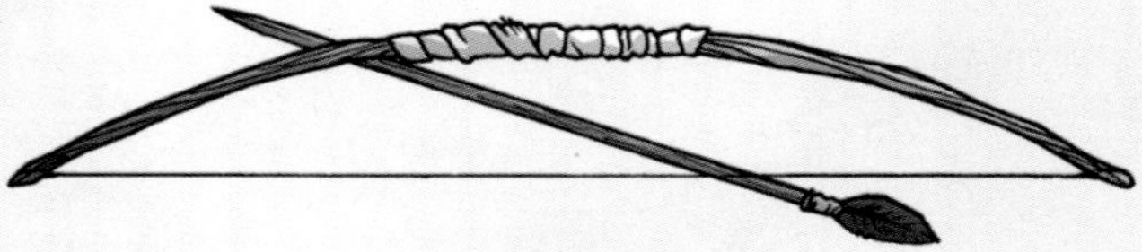

GO ON TO THE NEXT PAGE.

TWISTED JOURNEYS®

You take a moment to think about your answer.

WILL YOU . . .

. . . recommend that Mr. Balozi arrest them for poaching?

TURN TO PAGE 26.

. . . suggest that Mr. Balozi let them off with a warning?

TURN TO PAGE 33.

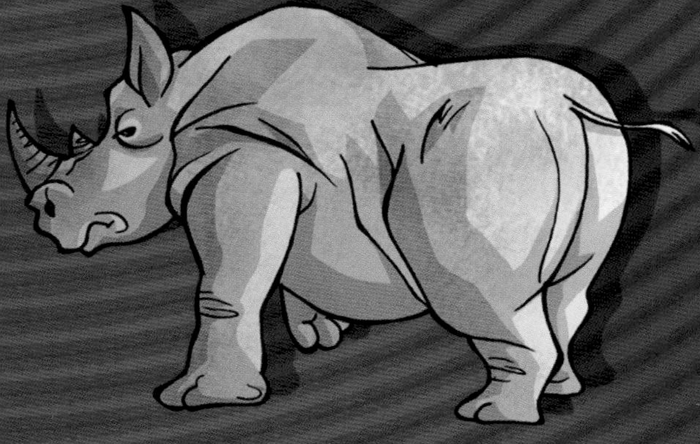

After a short drive, you get out and follow Mr. Balozi to a stand of odd-looking plants. "They look like a cross between a fern, a cactus, and a pineapple!" you exclaim.

"That's a very good description!" he says. "They're cycads, a type of primitive plant that was among the first plants to grow on land before the time of the dinosaurs."

"Why would anyone poach them?" you ask.

"They sell the seeds or even the plants themselves to private collectors." He shakes his head. "Endangered plants don't get the publicity that animals like elephants and rhinos do, but they're just as important to the ecosystem."

You pull out your camera. "I bet no one in my class has ever seen one of these!"

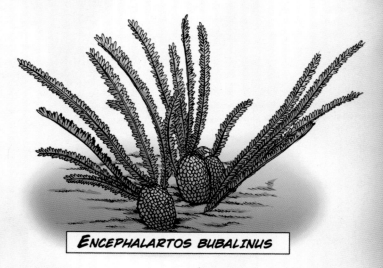

ENCEPHALARTOS BUBALINUS

THE END

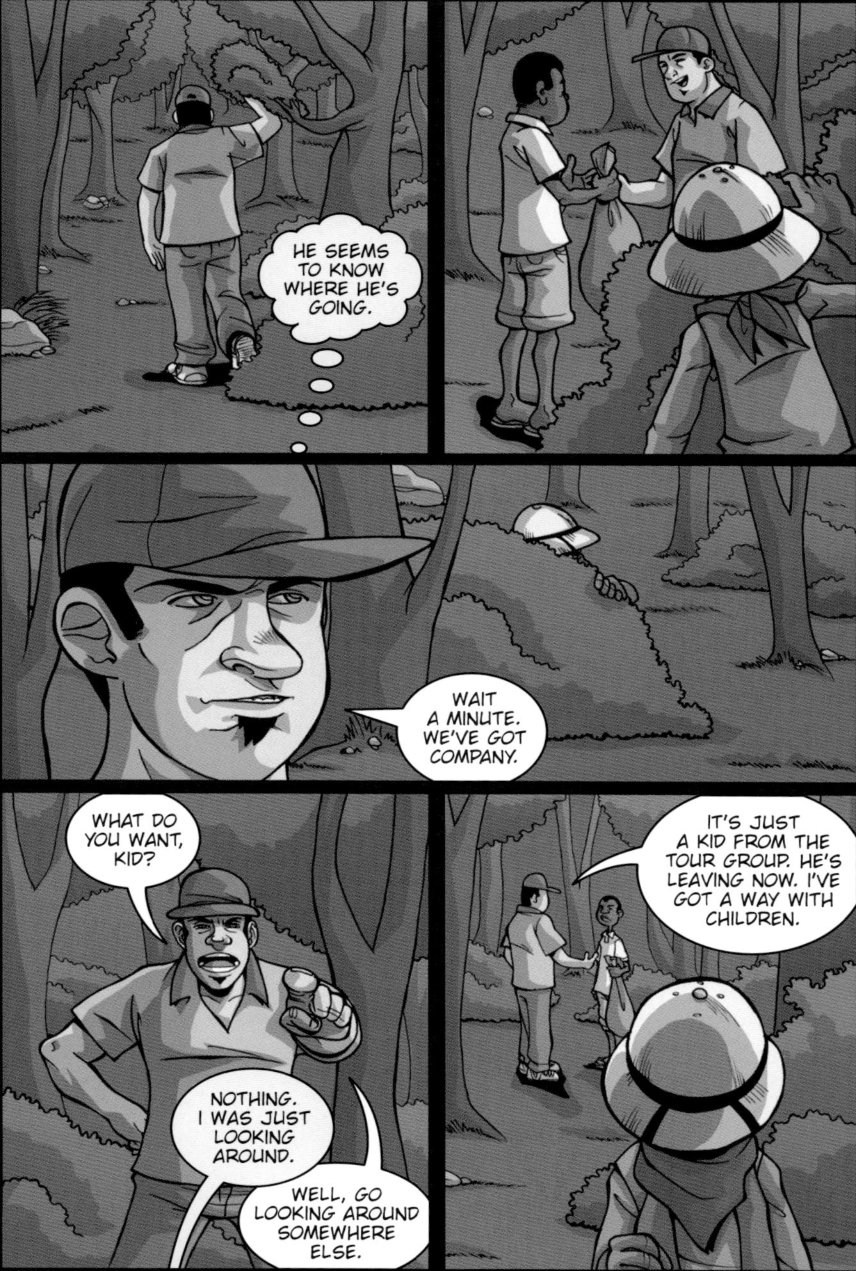
HE SEEMS TO KNOW WHERE HE'S GOING.
WAIT A MINUTE. WE'VE GOT COMPANY.
WHAT DO YOU WANT, KID?
NOTHING. I WAS JUST LOOKING AROUND.
WELL, GO LOOKING AROUND SOMEWHERE ELSE.
IT'S JUST A KID FROM THE TOUR GROUP. HE'S LEAVING NOW. I'VE GOT A WAY WITH CHILDREN.

GO ON TO THE NEXT PAGE.

You're pretty sure something illegal is going on, but Mr. Shelton looks mean.

WILL YOU . . .

. . . go exploring in a different direction?
TURN TO PAGE 14.

. . . confront these men about their suspicious activity?
TURN TO PAGE 78.

. . . head straight back to the rest area and alert Endesha?
TURN TO PAGE 58.

The balloon gradually drifts downward, and soon the basket is brushing the treetops.

It looks as if you could easily grab a fistful of leaves. "Hey!" says Endesha as you start to lean out. You think he's going to try to stop you, but instead, he gets a grip around your waist and says, "Okay, try it now!"

It takes a few tries, but you finally manage to pull a branch toward you and pluck a few leaves. As you let go, the branch snaps back into place and startles a flock of small, brightly colored birds that rise squawking into the sky. It's a sight you'll never forget, even if you live to be a hundred.

"Thanks, Endesha," you say. "This was the best surprise ever."

THE END

You manage to get your water bottle and sneak out of camp without being seen and set out toward the wooded area. It's farther away than it looked on the map. The morning is already getting hot, but your hat is keeping the sun off your face. It doesn't take long to drink your whole bottle of water.

After several hours, you finally reach the woods. You're glad to be here. It's cooler in the shade. Before you go looking for animals, you realize you should find some more water.

GO ON TO THE NEXT PAGE.

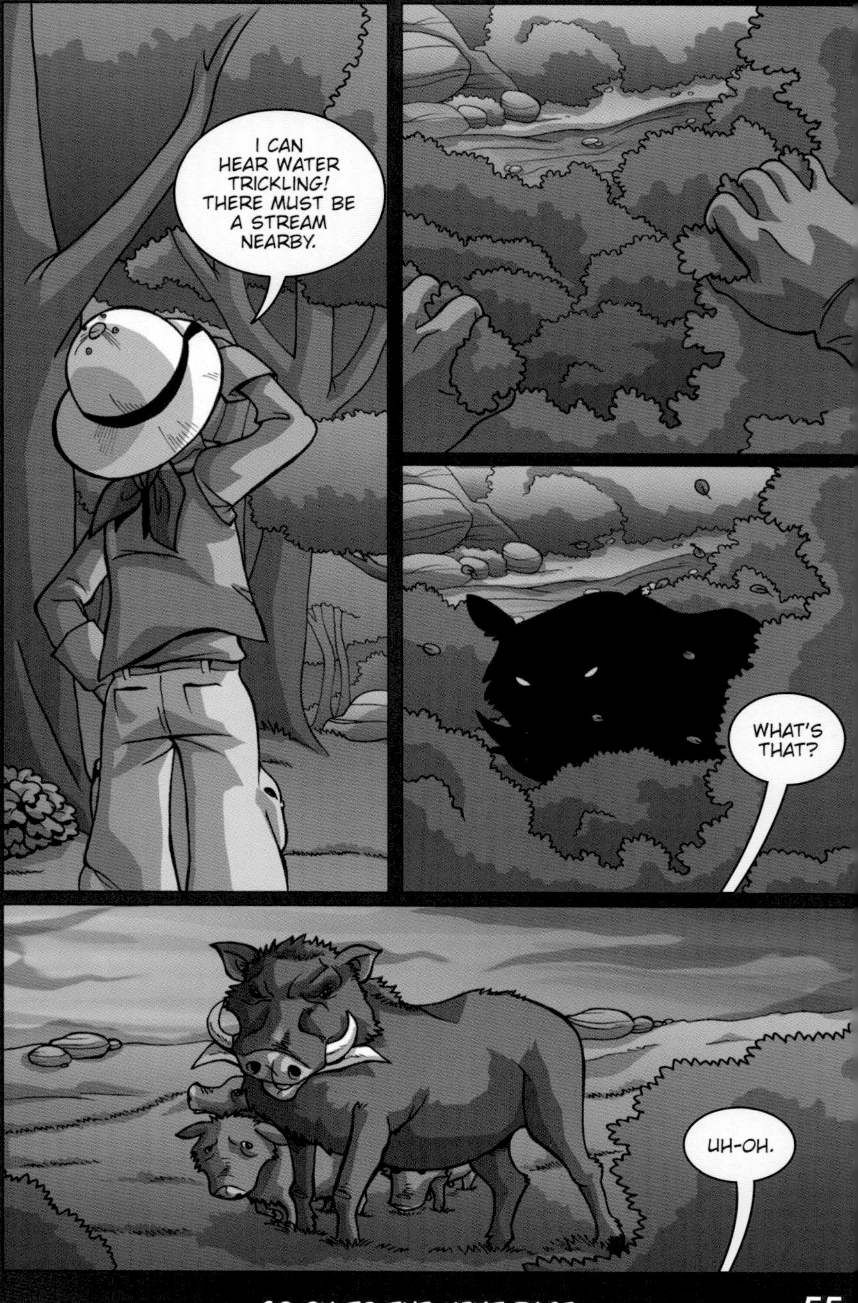
I CAN HEAR WATER TRICKLING! THERE MUST BE A STREAM NEARBY.
WHAT'S THAT?
UH-OH.

GO ON TO THE NEXT PAGE.

TWISTED JOURNEYS®

The mother warthog doesn't want you to get any closer to her—or her babies.

WILL YOU . . .

. . . avoid antagonizing an angry animal and seek water elsewhere?

TURN TO PAGE 88.

. . . ignore the threat from the warthog and get the water you need from the stream?

TURN TO PAGE 110.

Lake Victoria
Kenya
Serengeti
TANZAN

You're now up high enough that you can see right down into the site where the archaeologists are working. Some of them are using trowels to dig in the ground, while others are carefully brushing dirt from objects they've dug up. You lean forward and suddenly lose your balance. You flail with your arms in the air but to no avail.

As you tumble down the slope, loose rocks begin to tumble along with you. You close your eyes and throw your arms over your face, hoping to shield yourself from the avalanche.

When you reach the bottom of the slope, you open your eyes very carefully. Miraculously, you only suffered a few minor scrapes. When you look around, however, you realize that the rockslide sent a cascade of rocks and dirt all over the dig, ruining the archaeologists' work. A group of angry workers are standing around you in a circle, yelling at you in a language you can't understand.

You protest that it wasn't your fault, but that doesn't keep you from being deported from the country in disgrace.

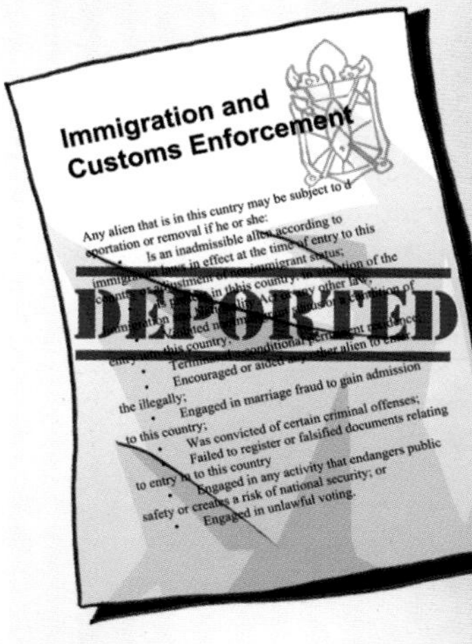
Immigration and
Customs Enforcement
DEPORTED

THE END

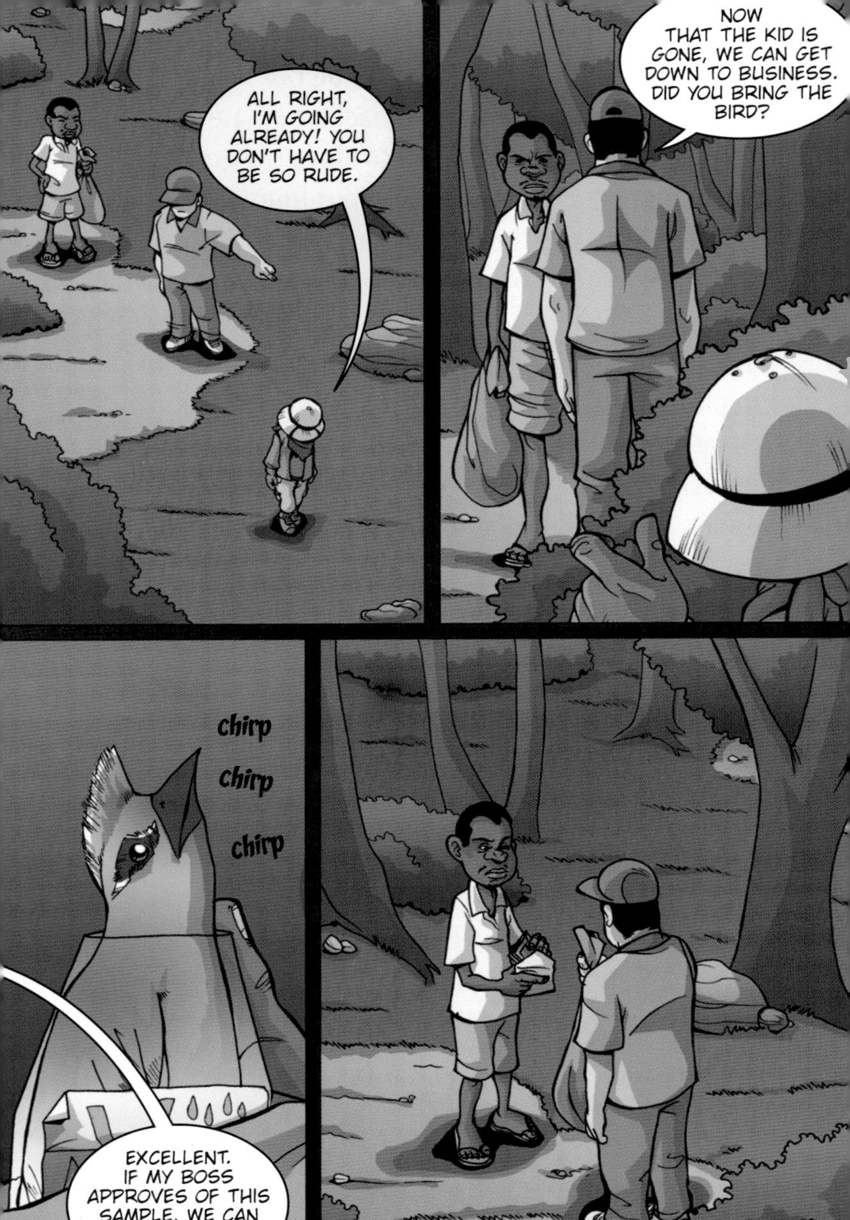
ALL RIGHT, I'M GOING ALREADY! YOU DON'T HAVE TO BE SO RUDE.
NOW THAT THE KID IS GONE, WE CAN GET DOWN TO BUSINESS. DID YOU BRING THE BIRD?
chirp
chirp
chirp
EXCELLENT. IF MY BOSS APPROVES OF THIS SAMPLE, WE CAN DO A LOT MORE BUSINESS.

You run as fast as you can toward the rest area. "Endesha!" you shout as soon as you're close enough to be heard.

Endesha comes toward you. "Whoa! What's wrong?" he asks.

"I just saw Mr. Shelton buying a bird from a local guy. They were acting like it was a big secret."

Endesha looks alarmed. "Tell me exactly what you saw." You tell him the whole story.

Endesha pulls out his cell phone and punches a speed-dial number. "Issa, have you got a minute? I have something for you."

GO ON TO THE NEXT PAGE.

A few minutes later, a jeep pulls up and Mr. Balozi, the wildlife officer you met earlier, gets out. At his request, you tell him exactly what you told Endesha.

Just as you're finishing, Mr. Shelton returns. Spotting the wildlife officer, he starts to walk away, but Mr. Balozi intercepts him.

"I'd like to see what's in that bag, please."

"Sure," says Mr. Shelton. He throws the bag at Mr. Balozi, pulling a hidden gun from his boot as he does so.

"Look out!" you begin to shout, but before you get the words out, Mr. Balozi draws his own weapon and fires. Mr. Shelton falls to the ground. Mr. Balozi kneels beside him, checking for a pulse and shakes his head.

Then he takes the bottle out of the bag and gently removes a little green bird. "Fly free, little one." He releases the bird. It chirps happily and then flies away.

Mr. Balozi smiles at you. "Did you hear that? The turaco was thanking you for rescuing him."

THE END

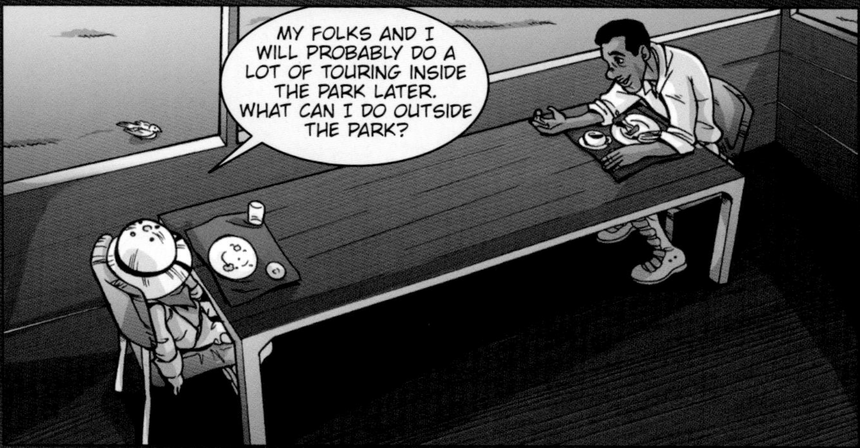
MY FOLKS AND I WILL PROBABLY DO A LOT OF TOURING INSIDE THE PARK LATER. WHAT CAN I DO OUTSIDE THE PARK?

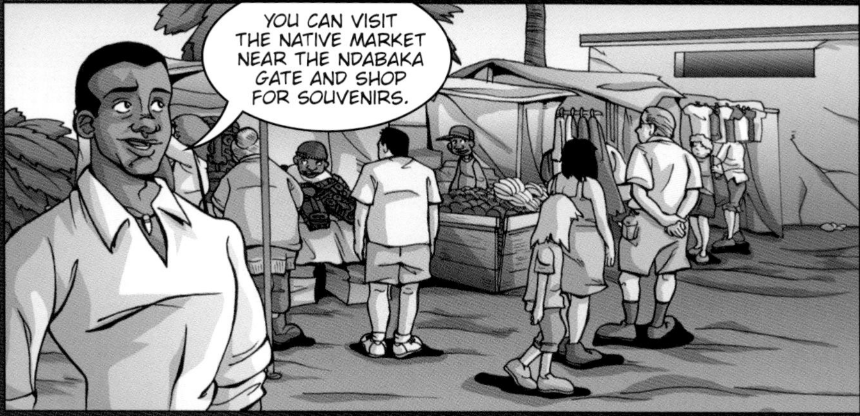
YOU CAN VISIT THE NATIVE MARKET NEAR THE NDABAKA GATE AND SHOP FOR SOUVENIRS.

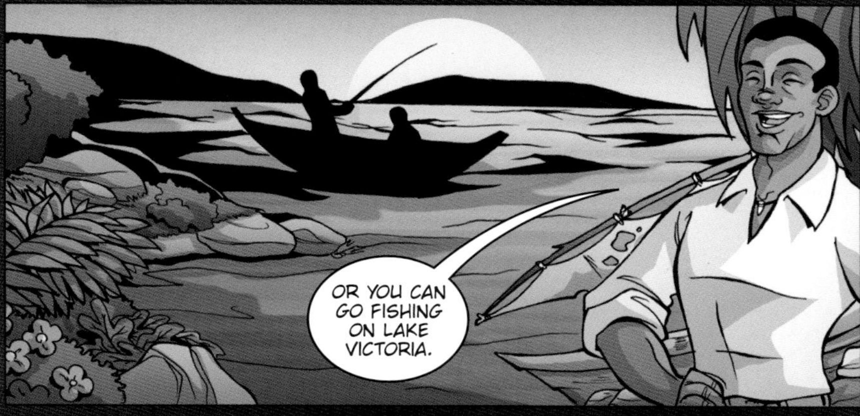
OR YOU CAN GO FISHING ON LAKE VICTORIA.

GO ON TO THE NEXT PAGE.

TWISTED JOURNEYS®

Which do you find more appealing?

WILL YOU . . .

. . . hunt for bargains at the native market?
TURN TO PAGE 39.

. . . fish in Lake Victoria?
TURN TO PAGE 76.

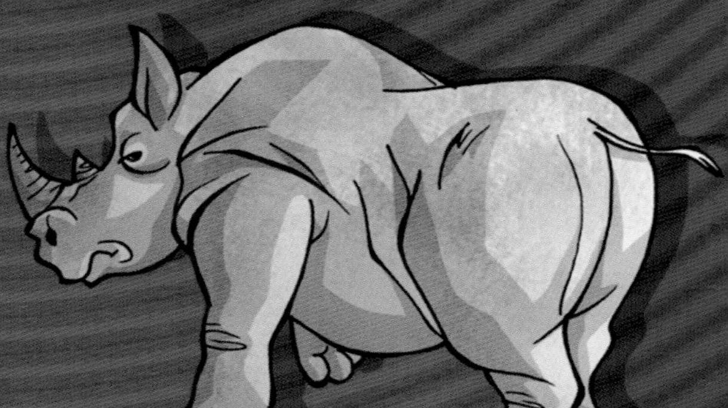

You dig into your wallet to see how much money you have. You are handing some bills to the dealer for a packet of topi meat when you hear a loud voice. "Police! Freeze!"

Mr. Balozi, the wildlife officer you met earlier, strides toward your little group. The dealer drops his backpack and starts running. The officer fires a shot into the air, and the dealer stops in his tracks. "You're all under arrest for trading in black market bushmeat," Mr. Balozi says sternly.

He looks at you. You try to stuff your wallet back into your pocket, but it's too late. "I don't like to arrest someone as young as you are," he says. "Maybe the magistrate will just expel you from the park."

This wasn't the way you wanted to end your adventure.

THE END

The other passengers agree with you that the chance to visit the Olduvai Gorge is a once-in-a-lifetime opportunity.

"Can we go into the actual dig and help the archaeologists?" asks one of the other passengers.

"No, ma'am, I'm sorry," says Endesha. "It takes special training to do that kind of work, and we can't disturb the archaeologists. But we'll be able to visit the on-site museum, where we can get an excellent view of the excavations and see some of the discoveries up close."

GO ON TO THE NEXT PAGE.

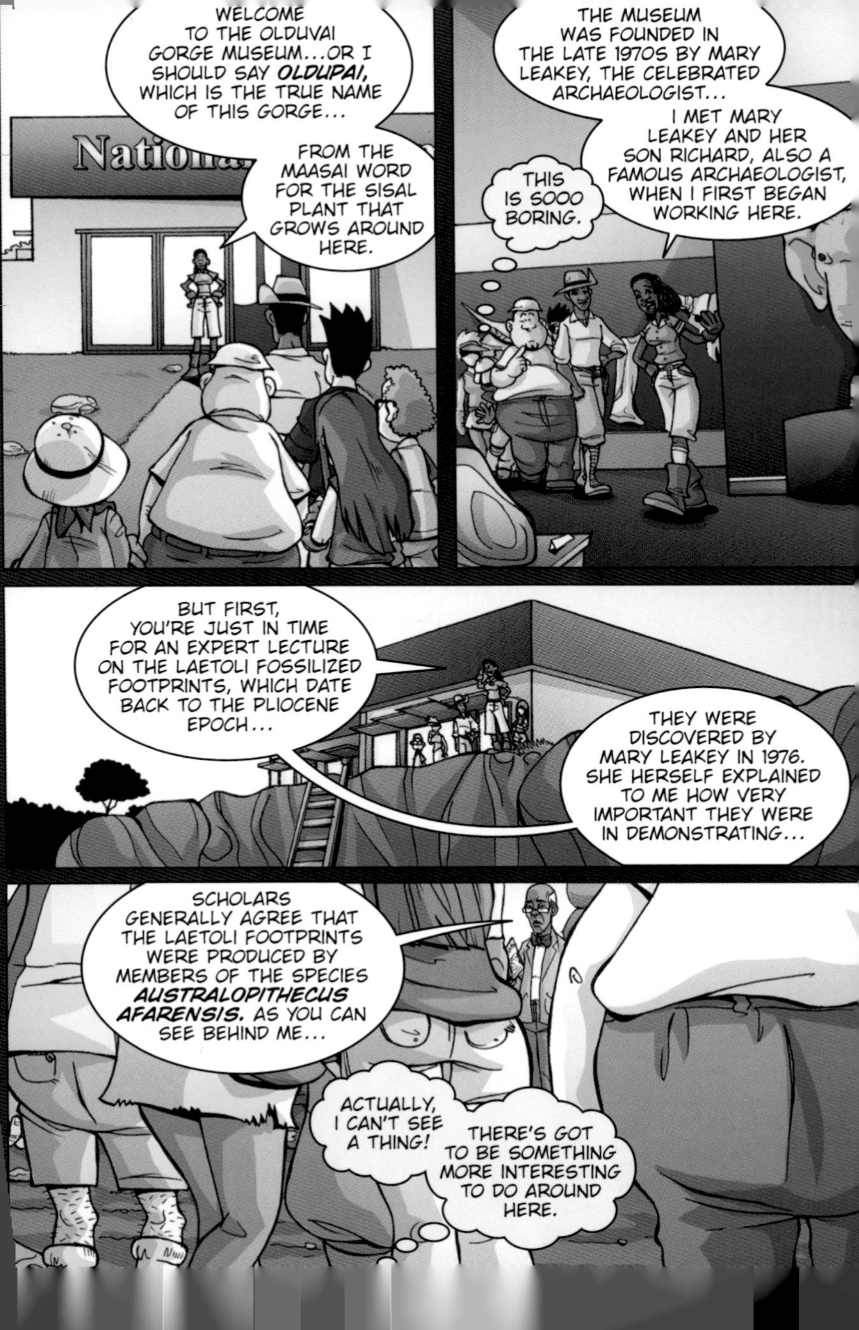
WELCOME TO THE OLDUVAI GORGE MUSEUM...OR I SHOULD SAY *OLDUPAI,* WHICH IS THE TRUE NAME OF THIS GORGE...
Nationa
FROM THE MAASAI WORD FOR THE SISAL PLANT THAT GROWS AROUND HERE.
THE MUSEUM WAS FOUNDED IN THE LATE 1970S BY MARY LEAKEY, THE CELEBRATED ARCHAEOLOGIST...
THIS IS SOOO BORING.
I MET MARY LEAKEY AND HER SON RICHARD, ALSO A FAMOUS ARCHAEOLOGIST, WHEN I FIRST BEGAN WORKING HERE.
BUT FIRST, YOU'RE JUST IN TIME FOR AN EXPERT LECTURE ON THE LAETOLI FOSSILIZED FOOTPRINTS, WHICH DATE BACK TO THE PLIOCENE EPOCH...
THEY WERE DISCOVERED BY MARY LEAKEY IN 1976. SHE HERSELF EXPLAINED TO ME HOW VERY IMPORTANT THEY WERE IN DEMONSTRATING...
SCHOLARS GENERALLY AGREE THAT THE LAETOLI FOOTPRINTS WERE PRODUCED BY MEMBERS OF THE SPECIES ***AUSTRALOPITHECUS AFARENSIS.*** AS YOU CAN SEE BEHIND ME...
ACTUALLY, I CAN'T SEE A THING!
THERE'S GOT TO BE SOMETHING MORE INTERESTING TO DO AROUND HERE.

The other visitors are fascinated, but you're bored. When Endesha's not looking, you sneak away from the group.

WILL YOU . . .

. . . look for a good place to take pictures?

TURN TO PAGE 80.

. . . get a better look at the archaeologists at work?

TURN TO PAGE 57.

. . . explore the steepest part of the gorge?

TURN TO PAGE 105.

You've only traveled a few miles when Endesha stops the vehicle and points silently to the left.

Ostriches! A whole flock of them are out grazing. Everyone starts snapping pictures.

Endesha explains that a flock of ostriches can also be called a pride, or a wobble.

"Do ostriches really hide their heads in the sand?" you ask.

Endesha chuckles. "Certainly not. They can defend themselves very well by kicking with their strong legs, and if that doesn't work, they can run at speeds over forty miles per hour. Only a very fast predator can catch them."

GO ON TO THE NEXT PAGE.

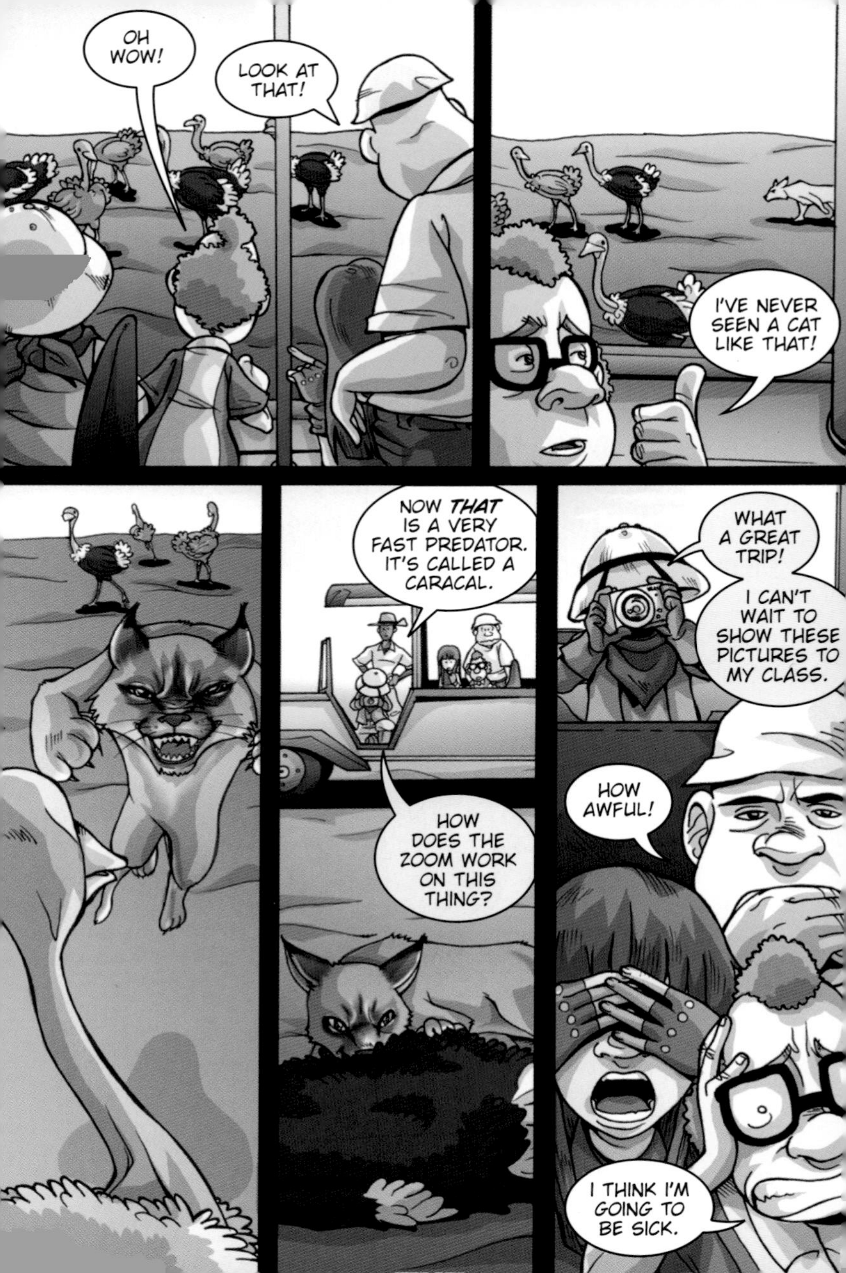
OH WOW!
LOOK AT THAT!
I'VE NEVER SEEN A CAT LIKE THAT!
NOW *THAT* IS A VERY FAST PREDATOR. IT'S CALLED A CARACAL.
WHAT A GREAT TRIP!
I CAN'T WAIT TO SHOW THESE PICTURES TO MY CLASS.
HOW DOES THE ZOOM WORK ON THIS THING?
HOW AWFUL!
I THINK I'M GOING TO BE SICK.

You're fed up with everyone trying to keep you safe. Just to show Endesha that you can take care of yourself, you take a few steps closer to get a better view. You peer over the edge and see black lava bubbling and spurting at the bottom of the crater.

The ground is really hot here, making you hop from foot to foot. Suddenly the mountain trembles and the ground under your feet tilts. You pitch forward and start sliding down the inside of the volcanic crater toward the pool of molten rock.

It's like the best roller-coaster ride of your life. Of course, it will also be the last.

THE END

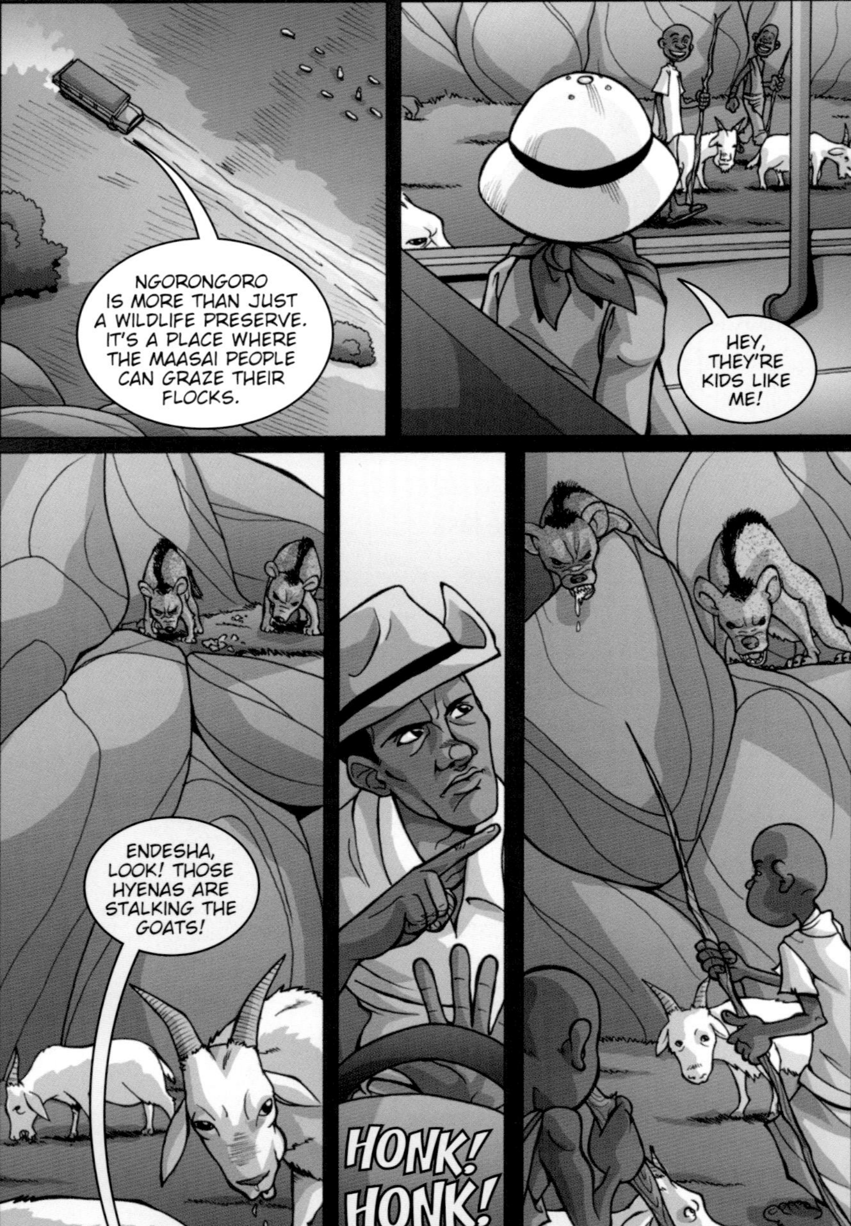
NGORONGORO IS MORE THAN JUST A WILDLIFE PRESERVE. IT'S A PLACE WHERE THE MAASAI PEOPLE CAN GRAZE THEIR FLOCKS.
HEY, THEY'RE KIDS LIKE ME!
ENDESHA, LOOK! THOSE HYENAS ARE STALKING THE GOATS!
HONK! HONK!

GO ON TO THE NEXT PAGE.

You are impressed by the courage of the Maasai herd boys. So are the hyenas, who slink off in disappointment.

One of the boys stays with the goats, while the other comes to the vehicle. "Thank you!" he says to Endesha.

Endesha points to you. "This is the one who first spotted the hyenas."

The boy turns to you. "Then it is you I should thank."

"You're welcome," you say. "I guess your folks would've been mad if you let anything happen to the goats."

The boy laughs. "That would have been the least of our worries. We would have been hungry! These goats are our livelihood. You did us a great service."

"Why don't I take a picture of all three of you?" suggests Endesha. "Mr. Johnson can watch your goats and fend off hyenas and porcupines."

You smile for the camera. One of the boys makes a funny face and the other one pokes him and you all laugh.

You may be halfway around the world, but kids are kids.

GO ON TO THE NEXT PAGE.

You say good-bye to your new friends and climb back into the safari vehicle.

"From here," says Endesha, "we can drive to the salt lake to see the flamingos or we can drive out to see the herds of wildebeest and zebra on the Salei Plain."

"Which do you recommend, Endesha?" asks one of the adults.

"Well, the flamingos are a spectacular sight. On the other hand, the Salei Plain is at its best this time of year. We're well into the calving season, and we might catch a glimpse of lions, cheetahs, or even hyenas stalking the herds. Either would be a fine choice."

GO ON TO THE NEXT PAGE.

WILL YOU . . .

. . . vote for the salt lake, to see the flamingos?
TURN TO PAGE 82.

. . . pick the Salei Plain, to see predators at work?
TURN TO PAGE 27.

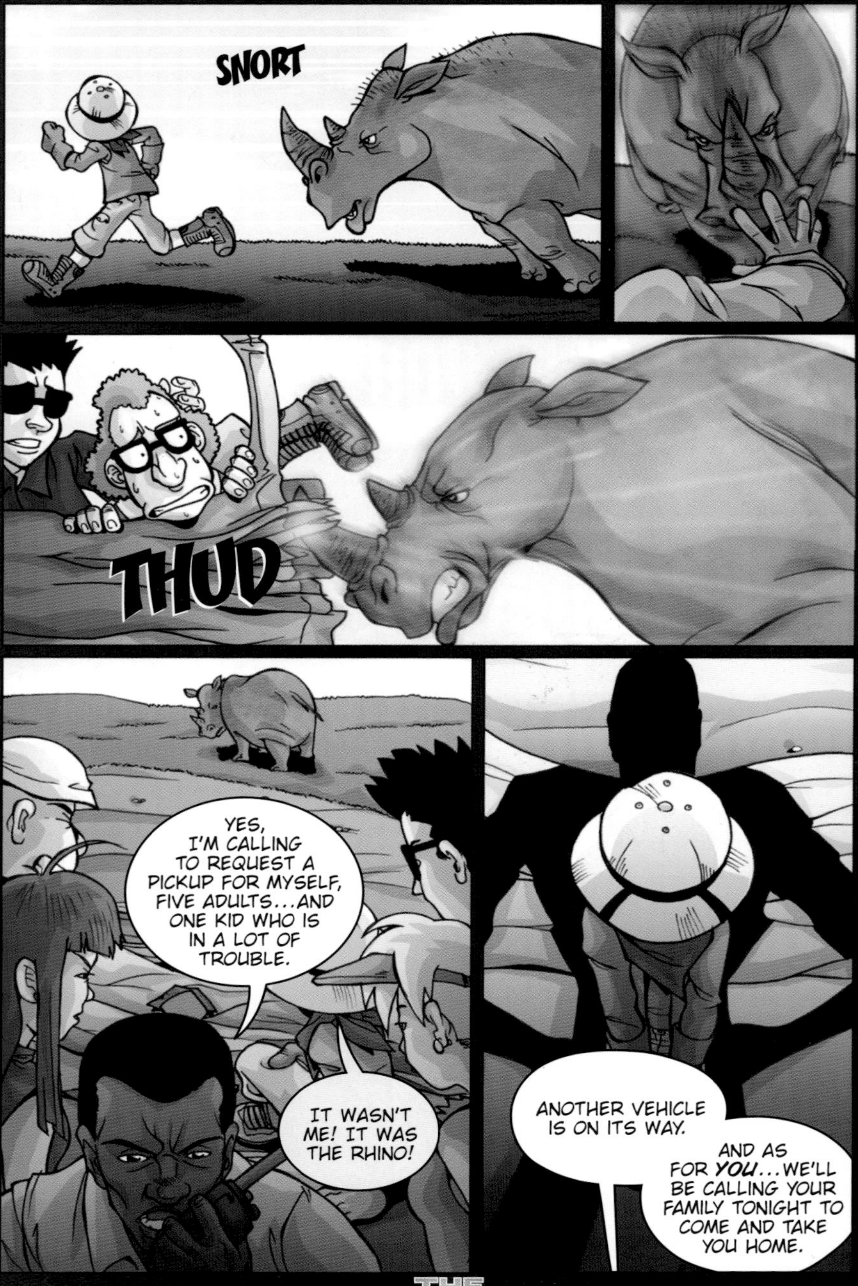
SNORT
THUD
YES, I'M CALLING TO REQUEST A PICKUP FOR MYSELF, FIVE ADULTS...AND ONE KID WHO IS IN A LOT OF TROUBLE.
IT WASN'T ME! IT WAS THE RHINO!
ANOTHER VEHICLE IS ON ITS WAY.
AND AS FOR *YOU*...WE'LL BE CALLING YOUR FAMILY TONIGHT TO COME AND TAKE YOU HOME.

THE END

"No thanks," you say. "I don't think it's right to eat wild animals from the park."

The others are just completing their transactions when you hear a loud voice. "Police! Freeze!"

You turn around and see Mr. Balozi, the wildlife officer you met earlier, coming toward you. The dealer look as if he wants to run, but Mr. Balozi has his gun out and the dealer thinks better of it.

"Trading in black market bushmeat is a criminal offense," Mr. Balozi says sternly to the adults. "You're under arrest."

He looks at you. "Were you going to buy any bushmeat?"

"No, sir," you say.

"He's telling the truth, officer," says one of the adults.

"This kid has a lot more sense than the rest of you," Mr. Balozi says. "You should be ashamed of yourselves."

And then you realize that for the rest of the day, you'll be the only passenger on the safari vehicle looking at the animals.

THE END

"I'd love to go fishing," you say. After all, it would be a change from just looking at animals!

Soon you're out on the lake in a sturdy fishing boat with a two-man crew. The boat has a heavy-duty fishing rod sticking out over the side from a built-in mount. The first mate explains that there are fish in this lake that weigh over 500 pounds. "So we use a 'big game' rig," he says. "This seat here, fastened to the deck, is called the 'fighting chair.'"

You're excited at first to be strapped into the fighting chair, but after an hour without a nibble, you unbuckle yourself and get up to stretch. The moment you sit back down, you get a bite! The fish fights back with surprising strength as you try to reel it in.

You struggle against the pull of the fish, wishing you'd had time to buckle yourself back in. "Would you like some help?" asks the captain.

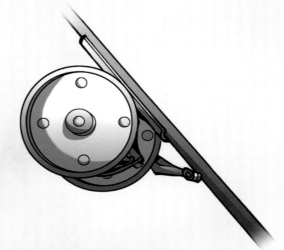

GO ON TO THE NEXT PAGE.

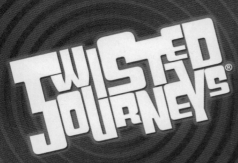

You really wanted to do this yourself, but you have to admit that this fish might be too big for you to handle.

WILL YOU . . .

. . . turn the captain down and do it yourself?
TURN TO PAGE 104.

. . . accept the captain's offer of help?
TURN TO PAGE 89.

Lake Victoria
Kenya
Serengeti
TANZAN

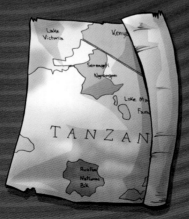

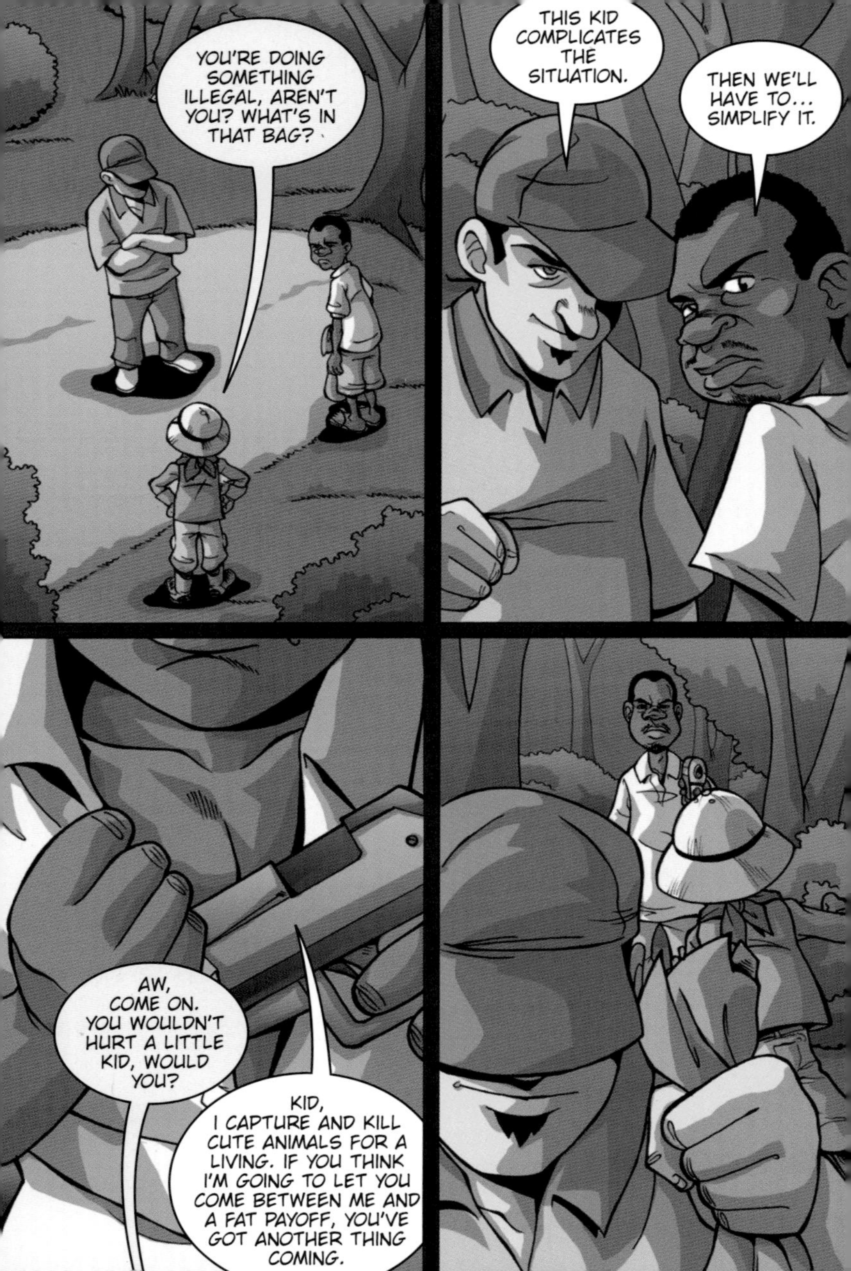
YOU'RE DOING SOMETHING ILLEGAL, AREN'T YOU? WHAT'S IN THAT BAG?
THIS KID COMPLICATES THE SITUATION.
THEN WE'LL HAVE TO... SIMPLIFY IT.
AW, COME ON. YOU WOULDN'T HURT A LITTLE KID, WOULD YOU?
KID, I CAPTURE AND KILL CUTE ANIMALS FOR A LIVING. IF YOU THINK I'M GOING TO LET YOU COME BETWEEN ME AND A FAT PAYOFF, YOU'VE GOT ANOTHER THING COMING.

You try to reason with the man as he marches you along. "You'll get caught, you know. The police will find fingerprints or something, and they'll figure out that it was you."

He chuckles. "Oh, don't worry about that, kid. When they find your body—if they ever do—the hyenas will have destroyed all the evidence."

It turns out that your African safari is going to be a lot shorter than you were expecting.

THE END

This whole area is bare and rocky with hardly any plants. It reminds you more of the moon than anywhere on Earth. You find a part of the ridge where you can see down deep into the gorge. It looks like a pretty good spot to take a picture. You step sideways to get a better angle.

Too late, you realize that this part of the ridge is unstable. The rocks all around your feet give way, and you find yourself caught in a rockslide.

When you finally roll to a halt, you sit up and look around. The first thing to catch your eye is the jagged end of a bone sticking out of your leg.

You stare at it for a few moments, wondering why it doesn't hurt more. Then you start feeling dizzy and everything goes dark. It hurts plenty when you wake up two days later, in a hospital bed. In traction.

You're pretty sure it won't be a comfortable trip home.

THE END

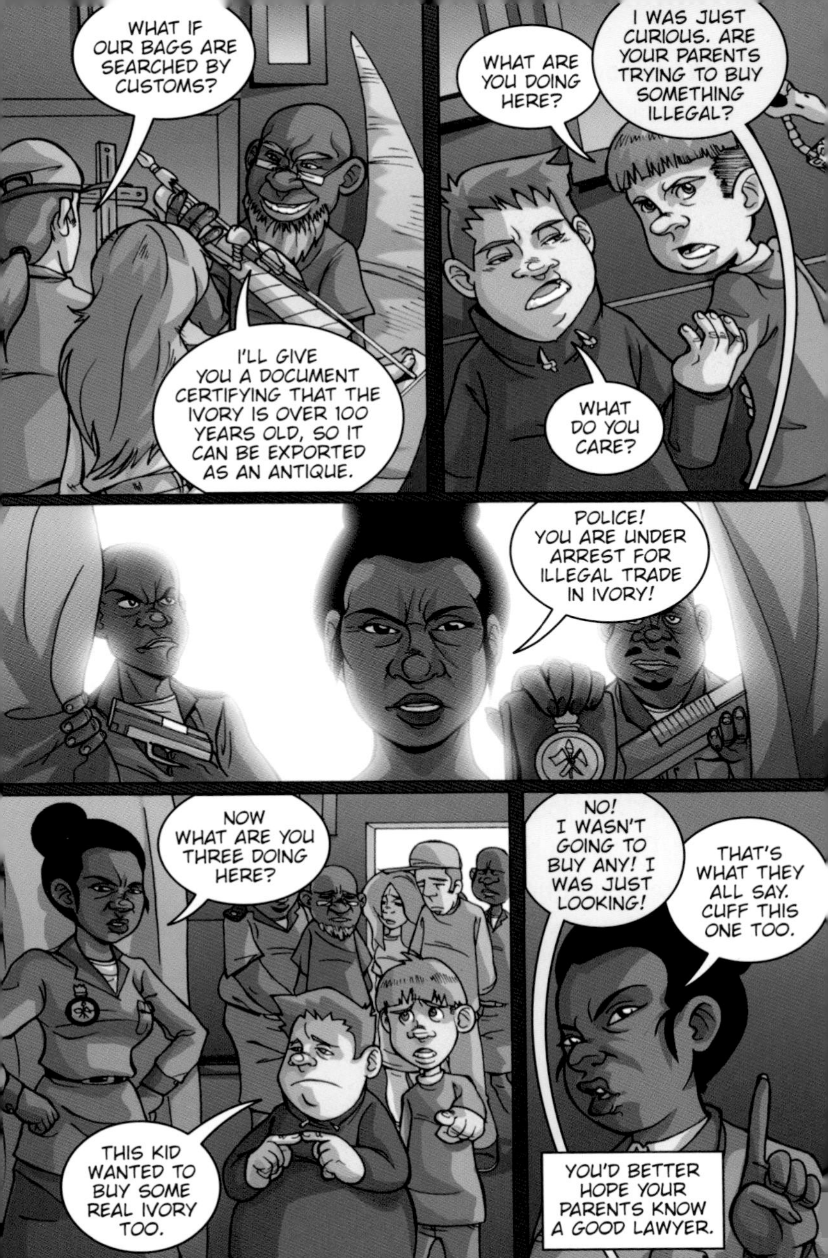

WHAT IF OUR BAGS ARE SEARCHED BY CUSTOMS?
I'LL GIVE YOU A DOCUMENT CERTIFYING THAT THE IVORY IS OVER 100 YEARS OLD, SO IT CAN BE EXPORTED AS AN ANTIQUE.
WHAT ARE YOU DOING HERE?
I WAS JUST CURIOUS. ARE YOUR PARENTS TRYING TO BUY SOMETHING ILLEGAL?
WHAT DO YOU CARE?
POLICE! YOU ARE UNDER ARREST FOR ILLEGAL TRADE IN IVORY!
NOW WHAT ARE YOU THREE DOING HERE?
THIS KID WANTED TO BUY SOME REAL IVORY TOO.
NO! I WASN'T GOING TO BUY ANY! I WAS JUST LOOKING!
THAT'S WHAT THEY ALL SAY. CUFF THIS ONE TOO.
YOU'D BETTER HOPE YOUR PARENTS KNOW A GOOD LAWYER.

When you get to the lake, your jaw drops. The water is covered with pink flamingos as far as the eye can see. Most of them are standing on one leg. Some of them are feeding with their bills down in the water. Others seem to be resting.

As you look more closely, you notice little flocks of fluffy white flamingo chicks here and there among the adults.

"Look at the baby ones! Why aren't they pink?" asks one of the adults.

"Flamingos are born gray or white," Endesha explains, "but they become pink from eating shrimp and algae that have pigments in them."

"Why are most of the flamingos standing on one leg?" asks someone else.

"It might be to conserve body heat," Endesha says. "No one is quite sure."

You walk away from the tour group to get a closer look at the flamingo chicks. Once you reach the far side of the lake, you notice some movement from among the trees at the bank.

GO ON TO THE NEXT PAGE.

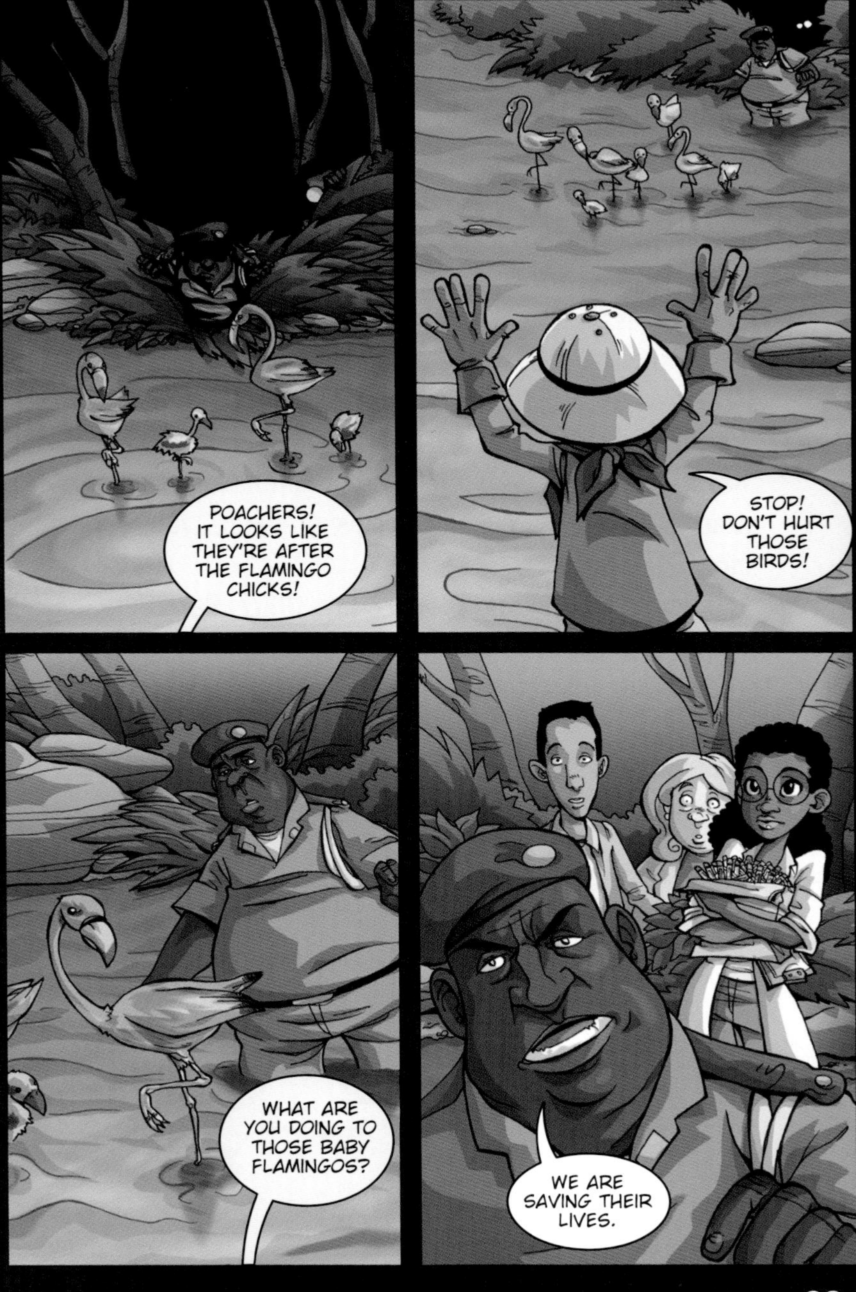
POACHERS! IT LOOKS LIKE THEY'RE AFTER THE FLAMINGO CHICKS!
STOP! DON'T HURT THOSE BIRDS!
WHAT ARE YOU DOING TO THOSE BABY FLAMINGOS?
WE ARE SAVING THEIR LIVES.

GO ON TO THE NEXT PAGE.

The man in the uniform introduces himself as Wildlife Conservation Officer Issa Balozi. "We're gathering water samples to test for dangerous bacteria," he says.

The female scientist looks at you curiously. "You thought we were poachers, didn't you?"

You nod sheepishly.

"That was a very brave thing you did, trying to protect the flamingos," she says.

"Brave and stupid and dangerous," says Endesha, sloshing over toward you. "If those *had* been poachers, they might have *killed* you! Or you might have been attacked by hyenas. Flamingos have predators, you know."

"Don't go too hard on the kid," says Officer Balozi. "I wish that all our park visitors cared about wildlife as much as this youngster does."

Somehow you feel both embarrassed and proud at the same moment. And the sight of thousands of flamingos all rising into the air at once is a memory you'll treasure forever.

THE END

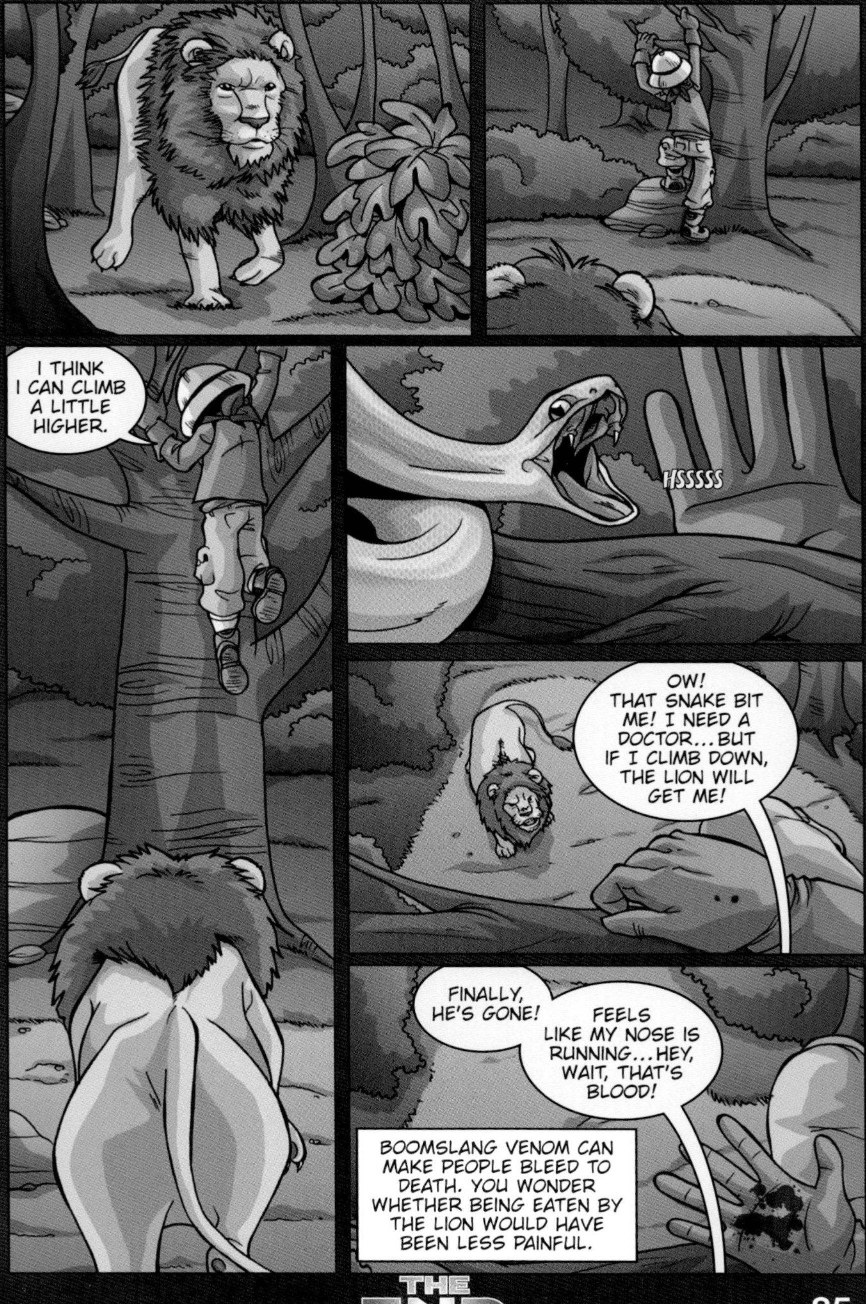
I THINK I CAN CLIMB A LITTLE HIGHER.
HSSSSS
OW! THAT SNAKE BIT ME! I NEED A DOCTOR...BUT IF I CLIMB DOWN, THE LION WILL GET ME!
FINALLY, HE'S GONE!
FEELS LIKE MY NOSE IS RUNNING...HEY, WAIT, THAT'S BLOOD!
BOOMSLANG VENOM CAN MAKE PEOPLE BLEED TO DEATH. YOU WONDER WHETHER BEING EATEN BY THE LION WOULD HAVE BEEN LESS PAINFUL.

THE END

When your airplane reaches Lobo, you find that Endesha has arranged a surprise for you: a balloon ride! You greet the pilot, a tiny black woman with short grizzled hair, and climb eagerly into the basket, followed by Endesha.

You've never ridden in a hot air balloon before. You're awed by the slow grandeur with which it rises and the glorious view that unfolds beneath you.

The pilot shows you the control mechanism. "Pulling this lever raises the level of the flame, causing the balloon to rise as the air inside gets hotter."

"How do you make it go down?" you ask.

"You just leave it be, and the balloon will descend gradually as the air inside cools." Then she steps back from the lever and gestures for you to take hold of it.

"Why don't you try being the pilot?"

GO ON TO THE NEXT PAGE.

TWISTED JOURNEYS®

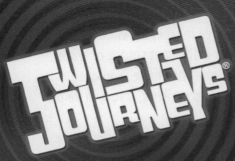

It's your choice!

WILL YOU . . .

. . . pull down the lever to make the balloon rise higher?

TURN TO PAGE 21.

. . . allow the balloon to drift lower?

TURN TO PAGE 53.

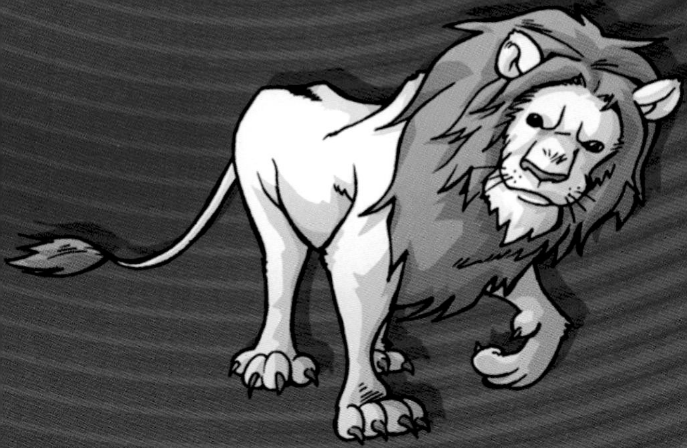

Rather than challenge a fierce mother defending her young, you decide to look for a different source of water.

It's getting awfully hot despite the shade. You get thirstier and thirstier as you keep walking, trying in vain to find another source of water.

Spotting a pile of leaves, you decide to rest for a while. It feels good to lie down. You watch drowsily as a line of ants marches along nearby.

Big ants. Lots of them. But they're still just ants, so you're not worried.

Fortunately for you, you succumb to dehydration before the ants discover you and begin to feed. You don't feel any pain as they swarm over you and eat you right down to the skeleton.

THE END

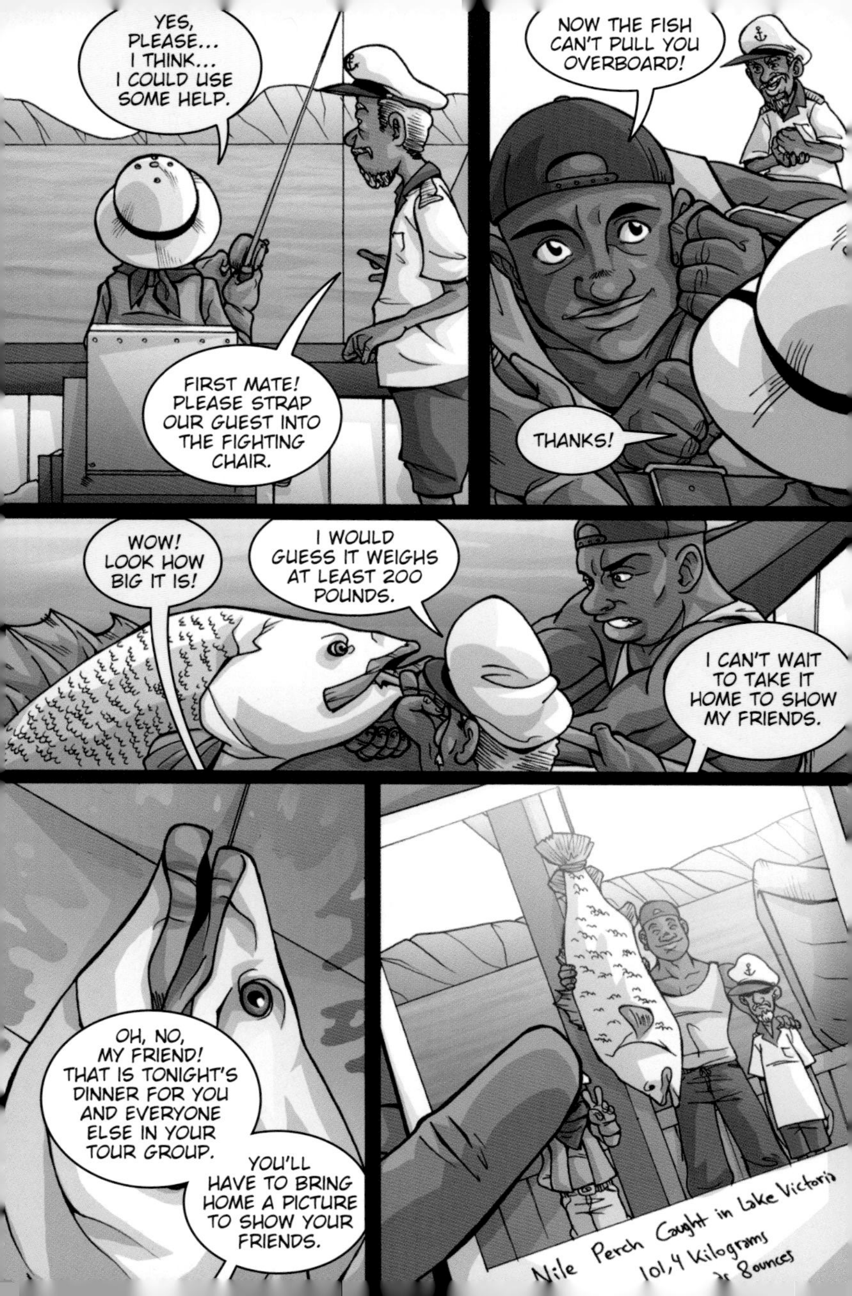
YES, PLEASE... I THINK... I COULD USE SOME HELP.
FIRST MATE! PLEASE STRAP OUR GUEST INTO THE FIGHTING CHAIR.
NOW THE FISH CAN'T PULL YOU OVERBOARD!
THANKS!
WOW! LOOK HOW BIG IT IS!
I WOULD GUESS IT WEIGHS AT LEAST 200 POUNDS.
I CAN'T WAIT TO TAKE IT HOME TO SHOW MY FRIENDS.
OH, NO, MY FRIEND! THAT IS TONIGHT'S DINNER FOR YOU AND EVERYONE ELSE IN YOUR TOUR GROUP.
YOU'LL HAVE TO BRING HOME A PICTURE TO SHOW YOUR FRIENDS.
Nile Perch Caught in Lake Victoria
101,4 Kilograms

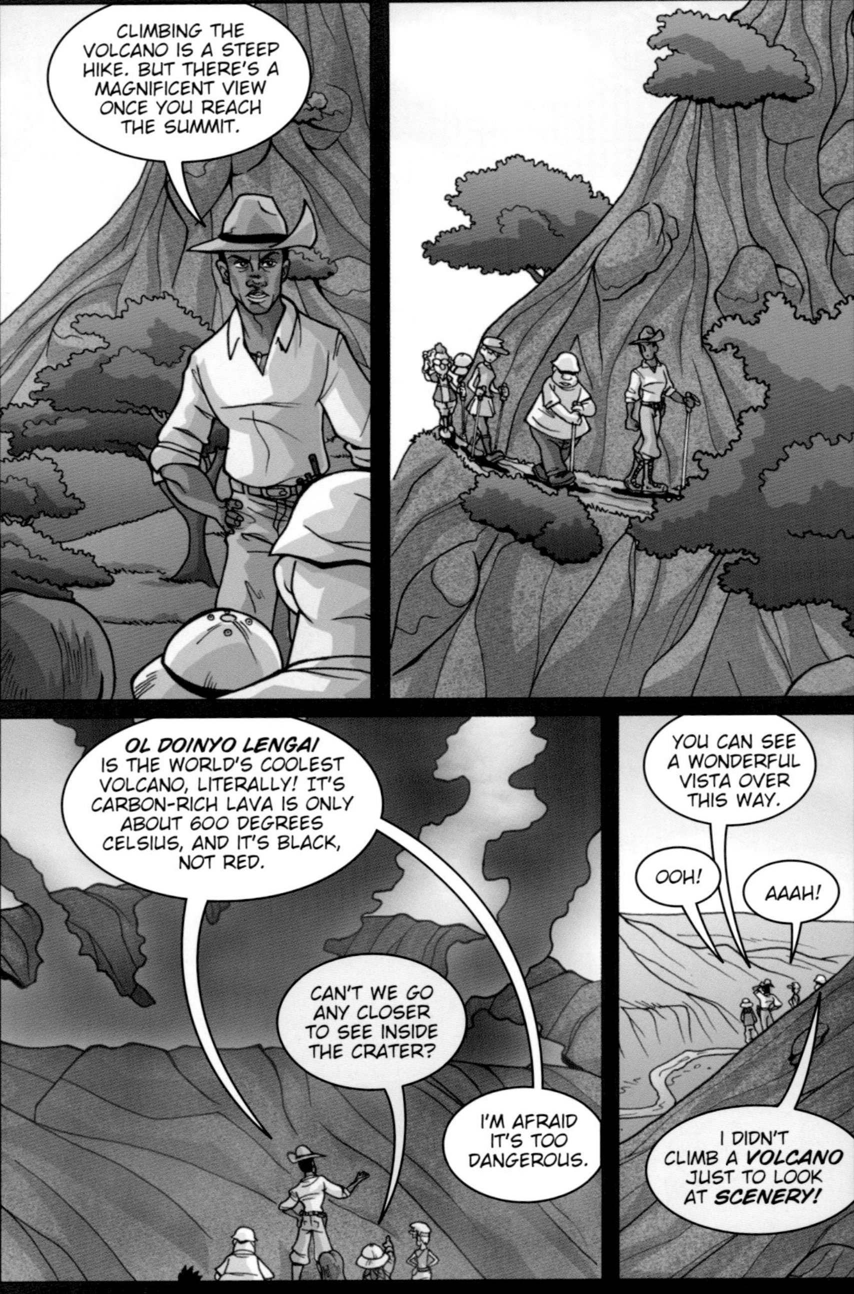
CLIMBING THE VOLCANO IS A STEEP HIKE. BUT THERE'S A MAGNIFICENT VIEW ONCE YOU REACH THE SUMMIT.
OL DOINYO LENGAI IS THE WORLD'S COOLEST VOLCANO, LITERALLY! IT'S CARBON-RICH LAVA IS ONLY ABOUT 600 DEGREES CELSIUS, AND IT'S BLACK, NOT RED.
CAN'T WE GO ANY CLOSER TO SEE INSIDE THE CRATER?
I'M AFRAID IT'S TOO DANGEROUS.
YOU CAN SEE A WONDERFUL VISTA OVER THIS WAY.
OOH!
AAAH!
I DIDN'T CLIMB A VOLCANO JUST TO LOOK AT SCENERY!

GO ON TO THE NEXT PAGE.

The rest of the group is looking at the view. Endesha's attention is taken up with pointing out elements of the scenery. Now is your chance!

You manage to duck away without being noticed and scamper up the gray, rocky slope toward the very edge of the crater.

You hear Endesha's voice from above. Rats! He's noticed that you're missing. "Come back here!" he calls.

GO ON TO THE NEXT PAGE.

TWISTED JOURNEYS®

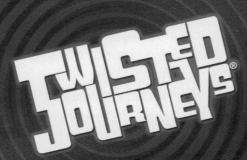

Endesha doesn't want you anywhere near that volcano crater!

WILL YOU . . .

. . . back slowly away from the rim?
TURN TO PAGE 35.

. . . try to get a closer look into the crater?
TURN TO PAGE 69.

Lake Victoria
TANZAN

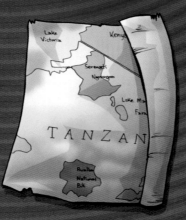

As you watch the huge wildebeest herd plodding along, you notice lots of mothers and calves.

Mr. Balozi looks through his binoculars. "They're progressing well," he says.

You spot a lone wildebeest calf several hundred yards away, trying to make its way back to the herd. Mr. Balozi points out a young cheetah hunkering in a nearby patch of long grass, intently watching the calf's movement.

"Shouldn't we do something to help the calf?" you ask.

Mr. Balozi shakes his head. "This is the circle of life, my young friend."

Suddenly the cheetah launches itself at the calf. The little wildebeest manages to dodge the attack. Putting on a burst of speed, it plunges into the herd. The cheetah slinks away to look for easier prey.

You clap your hands. "The calf made it!"

Mr. Balozi nods. "Hopefully it can find its mother in this big herd. If not, some predator may still be able to feed *its* family today."

THE END

"That's a great choice," says Endesha. "You'll have a great time."

As soon as you get back to your own tent after supper, you pack all of your gear. You do such a thorough job that you have to unpack to find your pajamas when it's time for bed!

The next morning, you're the first member of your family to get up. As soon as you're dressed, you run to the common area for breakfast, nearly bowling over Endesha as you skid into the buffet line. "Sorry, Endesha," you say.

"It's all right!" he says. "Don't worry. I won't leave without you."

GO ON TO THE NEXT PAGE.

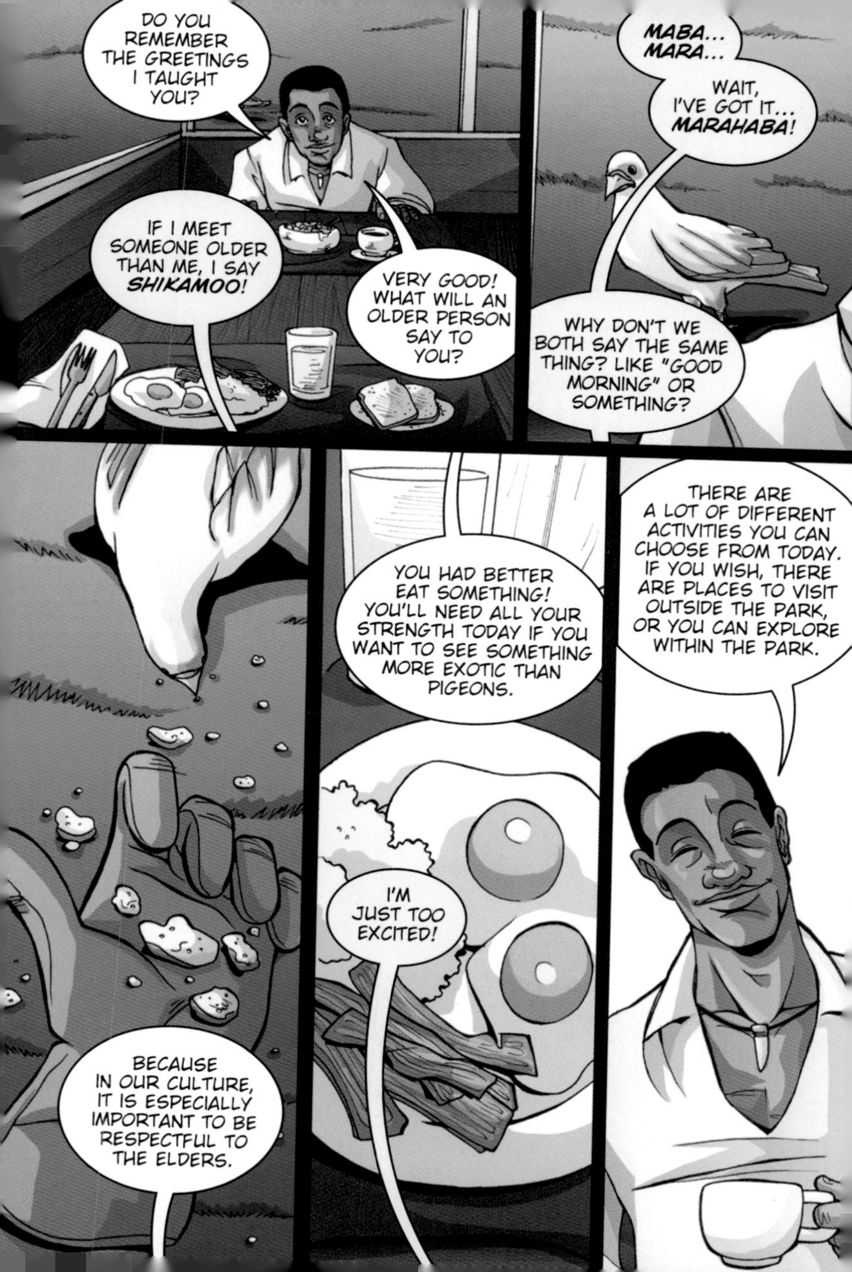

DO YOU REMEMBER THE GREETINGS I TAUGHT YOU?
IF I MEET SOMEONE OLDER THAN ME, I SAY SHIKAMOO!
VERY GOOD! WHAT WILL AN OLDER PERSON SAY TO YOU?
MABA... MARA...
WAIT, I'VE GOT IT... MARAHABA!
WHY DON'T WE BOTH SAY THE SAME THING? LIKE "GOOD MORNING" OR SOMETHING?
BECAUSE IN OUR CULTURE, IT IS ESPECIALLY IMPORTANT TO BE RESPECTFUL TO THE ELDERS.
YOU HAD BETTER EAT SOMETHING! YOU'LL NEED ALL YOUR STRENGTH TODAY IF YOU WANT TO SEE SOMETHING MORE EXOTIC THAN PIGEONS.
I'M JUST TOO EXCITED!
THERE ARE A LOT OF DIFFERENT ACTIVITIES YOU CAN CHOOSE FROM TODAY. IF YOU WISH, THERE ARE PLACES TO VISIT OUTSIDE THE PARK, OR YOU CAN EXPLORE WITHIN THE PARK.

Both choices promise interesting activities.

WILL YOU . . .

. . . visit the attractions outside the park?

TURN TO PAGE 61.

. . . explore the opportunities inside the park?

TURN TO PAGE 36.

You manage to slip out of the camp quickly and set off across the grasslands at a brisk pace. The woods are farther away than they looked on the map. You keep walking toward them, but they never seem to get any closer.

You feel the hot sun beating down on you, making your head ache. It also makes you terribly thirsty.

Now you're beginning to feel sick to your stomach. Maybe you shouldn't have had quite so many of those fried caterpillars.

GO ON TO THE NEXT PAGE.

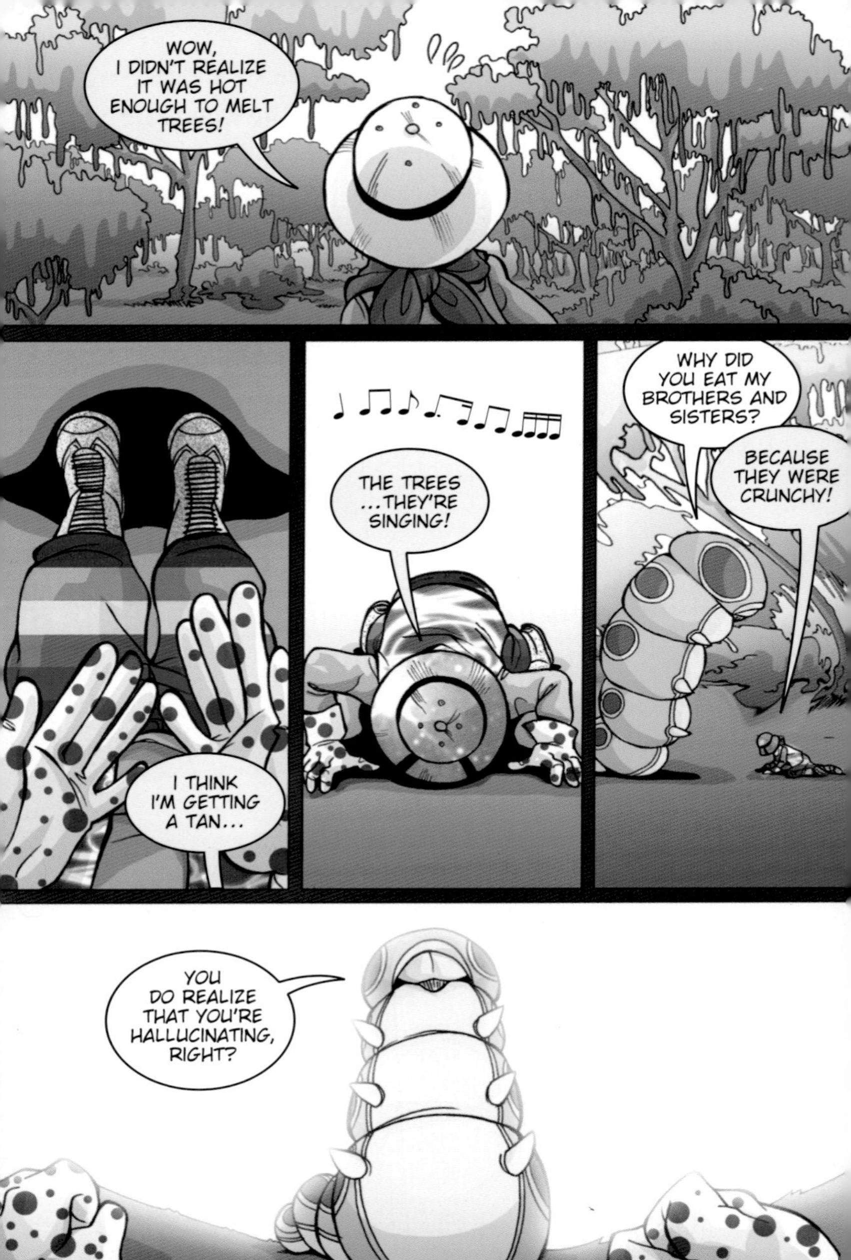
WOW, I DIDN'T REALIZE IT WAS HOT ENOUGH TO MELT TREES!
I THINK I'M GETTING A TAN...
THE TREES ...THEY'RE SINGING!
WHY DID YOU EAT MY BROTHERS AND SISTERS?
BECAUSE THEY WERE CRUNCHY!
YOU DO REALIZE THAT YOU'RE HALLUCINATING, RIGHT?

Now you know that hallucinations can be a symptom of heat stroke. Too late! It's the last thing you'll ever learn.

THE END

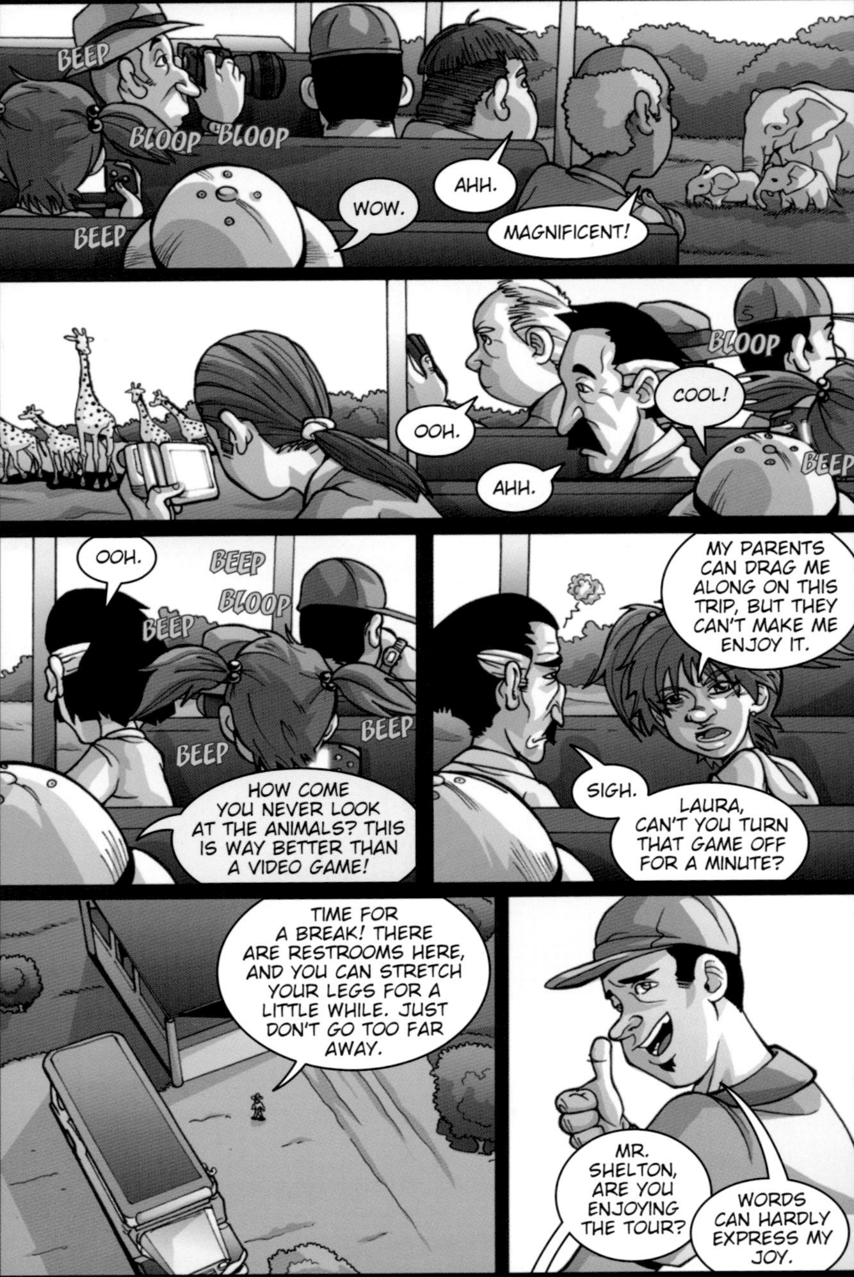
BEEP
BLOOP BLOOP
BEEP
WOW.
AHH.
MAGNIFICENT!
BLOOP
COOL!
OOH.
BEEP
AHH.
OOH.
BEEP
BLOOP
BEEP
BEEP
BEEP
HOW COME YOU NEVER LOOK AT THE ANIMALS? THIS IS WAY BETTER THAN A VIDEO GAME!
MY PARENTS CAN DRAG ME ALONG ON THIS TRIP, BUT THEY CAN'T MAKE ME ENJOY IT.
SIGH.
LAURA, CAN'T YOU TURN THAT GAME OFF FOR A MINUTE?
TIME FOR A BREAK! THERE ARE RESTROOMS HERE, AND YOU CAN STRETCH YOUR LEGS FOR A LITTLE WHILE. JUST DON'T GO TOO FAR AWAY.
MR. SHELTON, ARE YOU ENJOYING THE TOUR?
WORDS CAN HARDLY EXPRESS MY JOY.

GO ON TO THE NEXT PAGE.

When you come out of the restroom, you look around to see what everyone else is doing. Endesha has set up a little table with the cooler, a stack of cups, and a tray of cookies. He's relaxing in a folding chair nearby, drinking a glass of lemonade and fanning himself with his hat.

Laura has gone down to the lake. Mr. Shelton is heading off on his own, walking in a brisk, determined manner, with a messenger bag over his shoulder. The rest of the adults have wandered off, chatting.

GO ON TO THE NEXT PAGE.

TWISTED JOURNEYS®

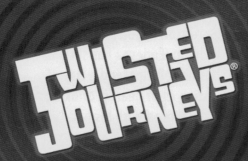

You're not sure what to do with your free time.

WILL YOU . . .

. . . follow Laura to the lake?

TURN TO PAGE 19.

. . . join the group of adults?

TURN TO PAGE 30.

. . . trail after Mr. Shelton?

TURN TO PAGE 51.

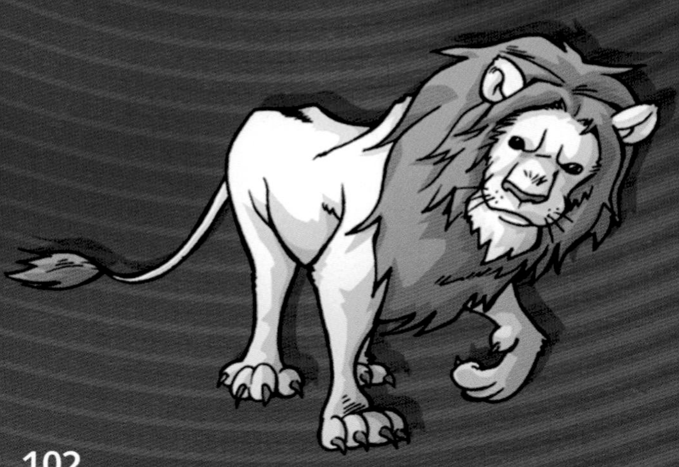

"What are those people doing down there?" you ask, pointing to the campsite.

Endesha looks through his binoculars. "That's a poaching camp!" he says excitedly. "The authorities have been using airplanes to try and spot them from the air, but the poachers hear the engines from a long way off and cover up quickly."

He pulls out his walkie-talkie and makes a quick connection. You try to eavesdrop, but the conversation is mostly in Swahili, punctuated with the occasional, "Okay, okay."

When Endesha signs off, he turns to you. "The poaching enforcement patrol is on their way now. They told me to thank you. If the raid is successful, they want to meet you and shake your hand in person."

You never imagined a simple balloon ride would make you a hero!

THE END

"No thanks, I can manage," you say, holding on grimly. Suddenly there's a tremendous jerk on the line, and you find yourself flying into the water, rod, reel, and all. For a terrifying moment the water closes over your head, but then you bob to the surface, gasping and spluttering.

The first mate hauls you into the boat. "Are you all right?"

You nod. "I'm sorry I lost the rod and reel."

"I'm glad we didn't lose *you!*" says the captain. "But now we must get you back to land."

"Why?"

"These lakes are infested with parasites. Without treatment you might develop snail fever."

"Does the treatment hurt?" you ask.

"I'm told it's relatively painless," the first mate says with a smile.

The captain is more serious. "The alternative is much worse. You start by getting a rash. Then you can get a fever, abdominal pain, bloody diarrhea . . ."

"Bring on the treatment," you say hastily. A parasitic disease is a souvenir you can do without.

THE END

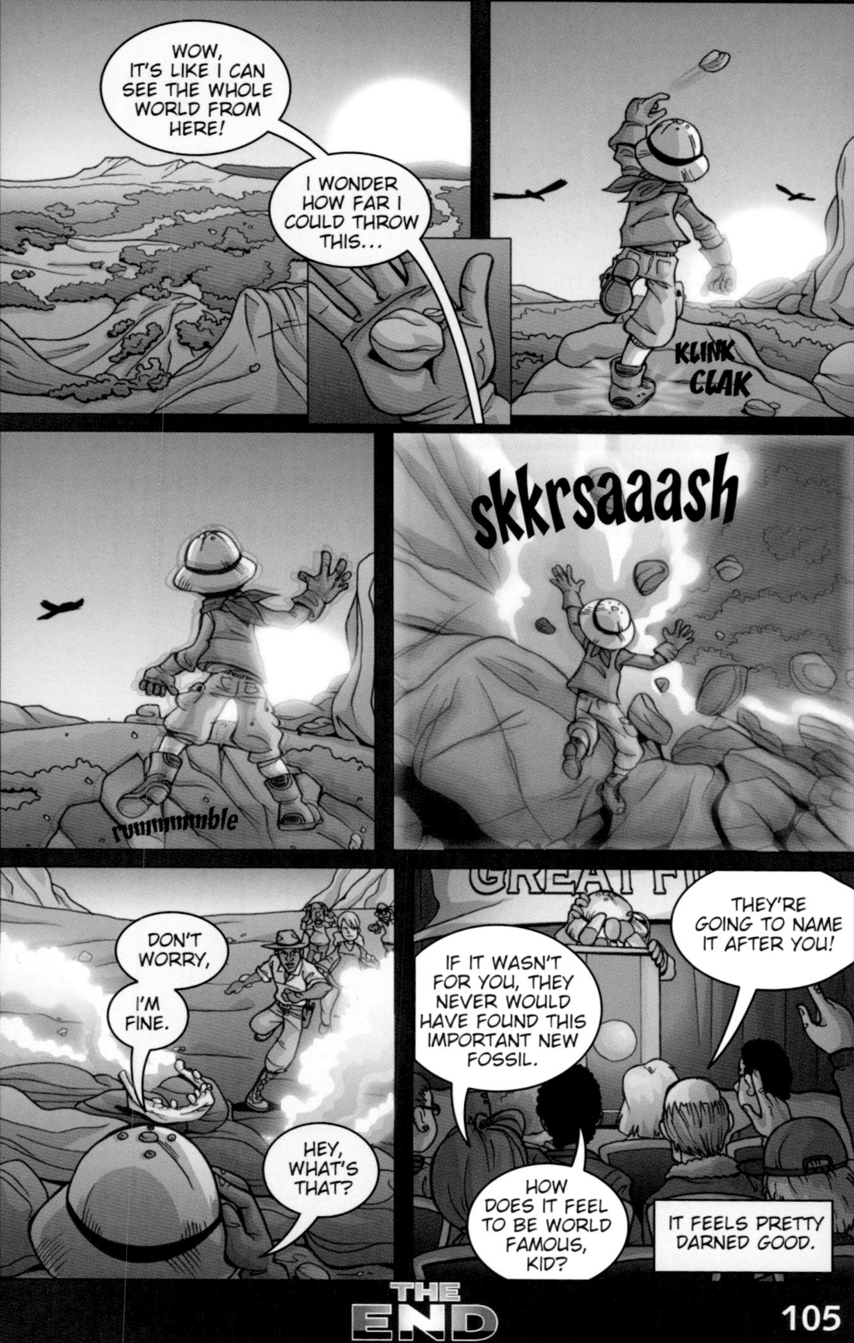
WOW, IT'S LIKE I CAN SEE THE WHOLE WORLD FROM HERE!
I WONDER HOW FAR I COULD THROW THIS...
KLINK
CLAK
rummmmble
skkrsaaash
DON'T WORRY,
I'M FINE.
HEY, WHAT'S THAT?
THEY'RE GOING TO NAME IT AFTER YOU!
IF IT WASN'T FOR YOU, THEY NEVER WOULD HAVE FOUND THIS IMPORTANT NEW FOSSIL.
HOW DOES IT FEEL TO BE WORLD FAMOUS, KID?
IT FEELS PRETTY DARNED GOOD.
THE END

"*Shikamoo,* Mr. Balozi," you say. "Thanks for letting us come along."

"*Marahaba,*" he responds, smiling. "It is my pleasure. Education is one of our most important investments in the future."

"There's one thing I'd especially like to know," you say. "What exactly does a wildlife officer do?"

"Wildlife officers do a lot of different things," says Mr. Balozi. "My special area is the prevention of poaching and smuggling. In other words, I try to stop people from killing wild animals to sell their meat, hides, horns, or tusks. I also try to stop people from stealing endangered plant or animal species."

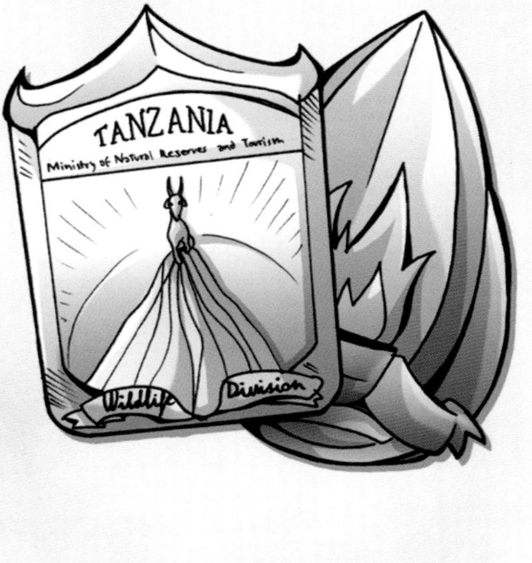
TANZANIA
Ministry of Natural Reserves and Tourism
Wildlife Division

GO ON TO THE NEXT PAGE.

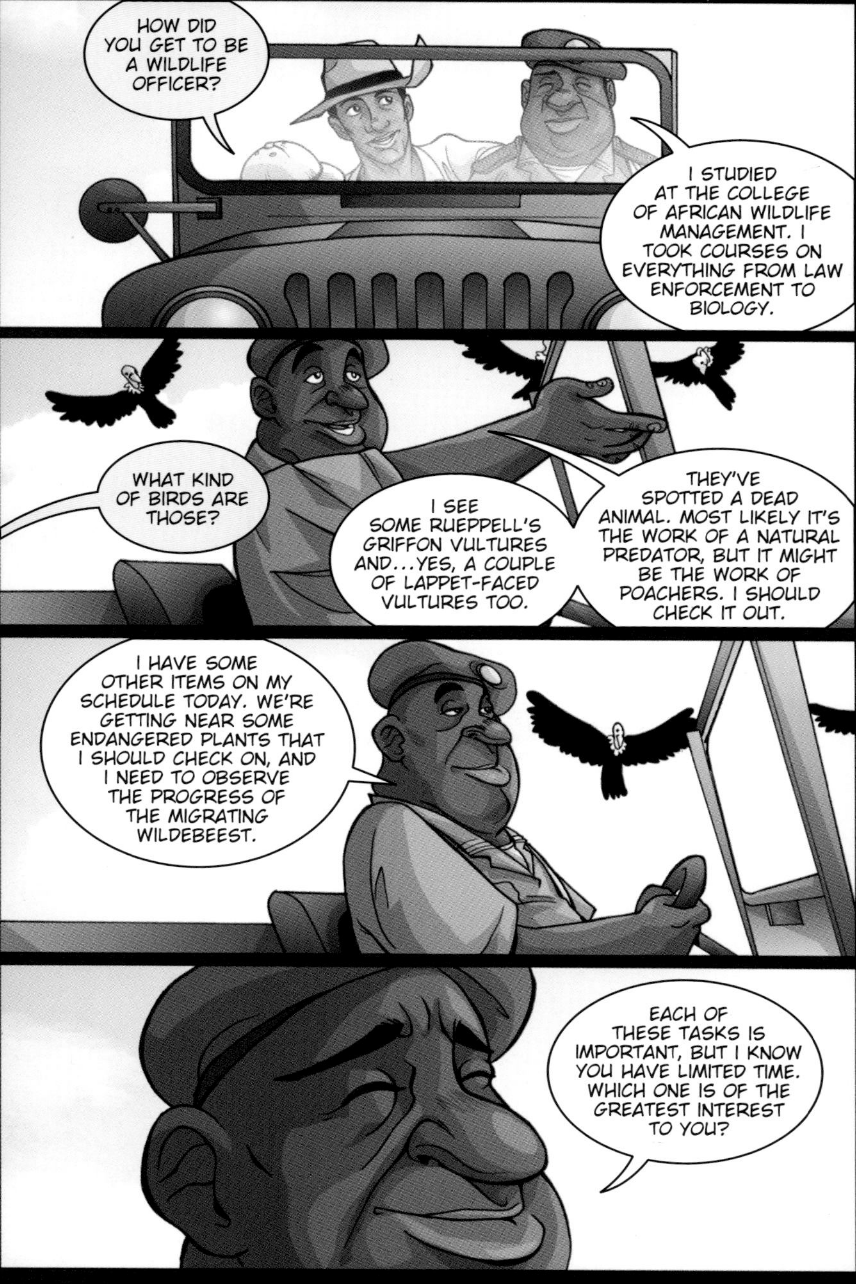
HOW DID YOU GET TO BE A WILDLIFE OFFICER?
I STUDIED AT THE COLLEGE OF AFRICAN WILDLIFE MANAGEMENT. I TOOK COURSES ON EVERYTHING FROM LAW ENFORCEMENT TO BIOLOGY.
WHAT KIND OF BIRDS ARE THOSE?
I SEE SOME RUEPPELL'S GRIFFON VULTURES AND...YES, A COUPLE OF LAPPET-FACED VULTURES TOO.
THEY'VE SPOTTED A DEAD ANIMAL. MOST LIKELY IT'S THE WORK OF A NATURAL PREDATOR, BUT IT MIGHT BE THE WORK OF POACHERS. I SHOULD CHECK IT OUT.
I HAVE SOME OTHER ITEMS ON MY SCHEDULE TODAY. WE'RE GETTING NEAR SOME ENDANGERED PLANTS THAT I SHOULD CHECK ON, AND I NEED TO OBSERVE THE PROGRESS OF THE MIGRATING WILDEBEEST.
EACH OF THESE TASKS IS IMPORTANT, BUT I KNOW YOU HAVE LIMITED TIME. WHICH ONE IS OF THE GREATEST INTEREST TO YOU?

GO ON TO THE NEXT PAGE.

TWISTED JOURNEYS®

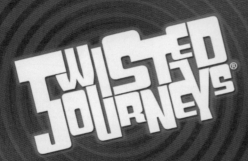

Here's your chance to see what it's like to be a wildlife officer!

WILL YOU . . .

. . . find out why the vultures are circling?

TURN TO PAGE 48.

. . . check out some endangered plants?

TURN TO PAGE 50.

. . . observe the wildebeest herd?

TURN TO PAGE 93.

Lake
Victoria
Serengeti
TANZAN

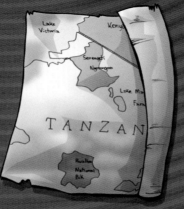

Remembering that rhinos have very poor vision, you drop to the ground and remain as still and silent as possible.

You hold your breath, watching as the rhino stands still, just a few yards away from you. It snorts a couple of more times. Then the rhino turns around and stomps away.

You let your breath out and get to your feet. A close encounter with a rhino isn't just the coolest thing that has happened on the trip. It's the coolest thing that has ever happened to you, period. You have a great story to tell your classmates when you get back.

THE END

You jump up and down, yelling at the top of your lungs. "Go away! Leave me alone!" Then you begin walking toward the stream. The mother warthog grunts loudly, and the three piglets break and run, diving headfirst into a nearby burrow. The mother dashes after them. When she reaches the burrow, she turns around and backs in, blocking the entrance and glaring at you.

The water is cool and clear. You take a long drink and feel a lot better. You refill your water bottle, get up, and look around.

From the edge of the trees, a male lion is staring at you. You slowly back away till you reach the base of a tree. You glance back nervously at the lion. He hasn't moved—yet.

GO ON TO THE NEXT PAGE.

If that lion charges you, you could be toast! You look up at the tree. Its branches are low enough that you could easily swing yourself up into it.

WILL YOU . . .

. . . remain at the base of the tree, watching the lion carefully?
TURN TO PAGE 46.

. . . climb as high as you can into the tree to get out of the lion's reach?
TURN TO PAGE 85.

TWISTED JOURNEYS®

WHICH WILL YOU TRY NEXT?

#01 CAPTURED BY PIRATES

#02 ESCAPE FROM PYRAMID X

#03 TERROR IN GHOST MANSION

#04 THE TREASURE OF MOUNT FATE

#05 NIGHTMARE ON ZOMBIE ISLAND

#06 THE TIME TRAVEL TRAP

#07 VAMPIRE HUNT

#08 ALIEN INCIDENT ON PLANET J

#09 AGENT MONGOOSE AND THE HYPNO-BEAM SCHEME

#10 THE GOBLIN KING

#11 SHIPWRECKED ON MAD ISLAND

#12 KUNG FU MASTERS

#13 SCHOOL OF EVIL

#14 ATTACK OF THE MUTANT METEORS

#15 AGENT MONGOOSE AND THE ATTACK OF THE GIANT INSECTS

#16 THE QUEST FOR DRAGON MOUNTAIN

#17 DETECTIVE FRANKENSTEIN

#18 HORROR IN SPACE

#19 THE FIFTH MUSKETEER

#20 PERIL AT SUMMERLAND PARK

#21 SAFARI SURVIVOR

#22 HERO CITY